In the arena, the slaves had worked rapidly; the fallen lion had been dragged away and the sands swept, leaving Tarzan alone again to face whatever Sublatus might send against him.

As the ape-man looked toward the far end, he saw six savage bull apes being herded through the gateway. They came from their cages filled with excitement and ferocity, surly and irritable from confinement and from the baiting to which they had been subjected. Before them they saw a hated man-thing, a Tarmangani like the ones who had captured them and teased them and hurt them.

"I am Gayat," growled one of the bulls. "I kill."

"Kill the Tarmangani!" barked the others, as the six lumbered forward.

And Tarzan stood alone to meet them, armed only with a puny dagger.

TARZAN NOVELS

MARS SERIES

ALL AVAILABLE FROM BALLANTINE BOOKS

TARZAN
AND THE
LOST EMPIRE

Edgar Rice Burroughs

BALLANTINE BOOKS • NEW YORK

To Jean Hulbert

ISBN 0-345-32957-0

This authorized edition published by arrangement with Edgar Rice Burroughs, Inc.

Printed in Canada

First U.S. Printing: October 1963
Fourteenth Printing: April 1988

Cover art by Boris Vallejo

1

NKIMA danced excitedly upon the naked, brown shoulder of his master. He chattered and scolded, now looking up inquiringly into Tarzan's face and then off into the jungle.

"Something is coming, Bwana," said Muviro, sub-chief of the Waziri. "Nkima has heard it."

"And Tarzan," said the ape-man.

"The big Bwana's ears are as keen as the ears of Bara the antelope," said Muviro.

"Had they not been, Tarzan would not be here today," replied the ape-man, with a smile. "He would not have grown to manhood had not Kala, his mother, taught him to use all of the senses that Mulungu gave him."

"What comes?" asked Muviro.

"A party of men," replied Tarzan.

"Perhaps they are not friendly," suggested the African. "Shall I warn the warriors?"

Tarzan glanced about the little camp where a score of his fighting men were busy preparing their evening meal and saw that, as was the custom of the Waziri, their weapons were in order and at hand.

"No," he said. "It will, I believe, be unnecessary, as these people who are approaching do not come stealthily as enemies would, nor are their numbers so great as to cause us any apprehension."

But Nkima, a born pessimist, expected only the worst, and as the approaching party came nearer his excitement increased. He leaped from Tarzan's shoulder to the ground, jumped up and down several times and then, springing back to Tarzan's side, seized his arm and attempted to drag him to his feet.

"Run, run!" he cried, in the language of the apes. "Strange Gomangani are coming. They will kill little Nkima."

"Do not be afraid, Nkima," said the ape-man. "Tarzan and Muviro will not let the strangers hurt you."

"I smell a strange Tarmangani," chattered Nkima. "There

is a Tarmangani with them. The Tarmangani are worse than the Gomangani. They come with thundersticks and kill little Nkima and all his brothers and sisters. They kill the Mangani. They kill the Gomangani. They kill everything with their thundersticks. Nkima does not like the Tarmangani. Nkima is afraid."

To Nkima, as to the other denizens of the jungle, Tarzan was no Tarmangani, no white man. He was of the jungle. He was one of them, and if they thought of him as being anything other than just Tarzan it was as a Mangani, a great ape, that they classified him.

The advance of the strangers was now plainly audible to everyone in the camp. The Waziri warriors glanced into the jungle in the direction from which the sounds were coming and then back to Tarzan and Muviro, but when they saw that their leaders were not concerned they went quietly on with their cooking.

A tall Negro warrior was the first of the party to come within sight of the camp. When he saw the Waziri he halted and an instant later a bearded white man stopped beside him.

For an instant the white man surveyed the camp and then he came forward, making the sign of peace. Out of the jungle a dozen or more warriors followed him. Most of them were porters, there being but three or four rifles in evidence.

Tarzan and the Waziri realized at once that it was a small and harmless party, and even Nkima, who had retreated to the safety of a near-by tree, showed his contempt by scampering fearlessly back to climb to the shoulder of his master.

"Doctor von Harben!" exclaimed Tarzan, as the bearded stranger approached. "I scarcely recognized you at first."

"God has been kind to me, Tarzan of the Apes," said von Harben, extending his hand. "I was on my way to see you and I have found you a full two days' march sooner than I expected."

"We are after a cattle-killer," explained Tarzan. "He has come into our kraal several nights of late and killed some of our best cattle, but he is very cunning. I think he must be an old lion to outwit Tarzan for so long.

"But what brings you into Tarzan's country, Doctor? I hope it is only a neighborly visit and that no trouble has come to my good friend, though your appearance belies my hope."

"I, too, wish that it were nothing more than a friendly call," said von Harben, "but as a matter of fact I am here to seek your help because I am in trouble—very serious trouble, I fear."

"Do not tell me that the Arabs have come down again to take slaves or to steal ivory, or is it that the leopard men are waylaying your people upon the jungle trails at night?"

"No, it is neither the one nor the other. I have come to see you upon a more personal matter. It is about my son, Erich. You have never met him."

"No," said Tarzan; "but you are tired and hungry. Let your men make camp here. My evening meal is ready; while you and I eat you shall tell me how Tarzan may serve you."

As the Waziri, at Tarzan's command, assisted von Harben's men in making their camp, the doctor and the ape-man sat cross-legged upon the ground and ate the rough fare that Tarzan's Waziri cook had prepared.

Tarzan saw that his guest's mind was filled with the trouble that had brought him in search of the ape-man, and so he did not wait until they had finished the meal to reopen the subject, but urged von Harben to continue his story at once.

"I wish to preface the real object of my visit with a few words of explanation," commenced von Harben. "Erich is my only son. Four years ago, at the age of nineteen, he completed his university course with honors and received his first degree. Since then he has spent the greater part of his time in pursuing his studies in various European universities, where he has specialized in archæology and the study of dead languages. His one hobby, outside of his chosen field, has been mountain climbing and during succeeding summer vacations he scaled every important Alpine peak.

"A few months ago he came here to visit me at the mission and immediately became interested in the study of the various Bantu dialects that are in use by the several tribes in our district and those adjacent thereto.

"While pursuing his investigation among the natives he ran across that old legend of The Lost Tribe of the Wiramwazi Mountains, with which we are all so familiar. Immediately his mind became imbued, as have the minds of so many others, with the belief that this fable might have originated in fact and that if he could trace it down he might possibly find descendants of one of the lost tribes of Biblical history."

"I know the legend well," said Tarzan, "and because it is so persistent and the details of its narration by the natives so circumstantial, I have thought that I should like to investigate it myself, but in the past no necessity has arisen to take me close to the Wiramwazi Mountains."

"I must confess," continued the doctor, "that I also have had the same urge many times. I have upon two occasions talked with men of the Bagego tribe that live upon the slopes of the Wiramwazi Mountains and in both instances I have been assured that a tribe of white men dwells somewhere in the depths of that great mountain range. Both of these men told me that their tribe has carried on trade with these people from time immemorial and each assured me that he had often seen members of The Lost Tribe both upon occasions of peaceful trading and during the warlike raids that the mountaineers occasionally launched upon the Bagego.

"The result was that when Erich suggested an expedition to the Wiramwazi I rather encouraged him, since he was well fitted to undertake the adventure. His knowledge of Bantu and his intensive, even though brief, experience among the natives gave him an advantage that few scholars otherwise equipped by education to profit by such an expedition would have, while his considerable experience as a mountain climber would, I felt, stand him in good stead during such an adventure.

"On the whole I felt that he was an ideal man to lead such an expedition, and my only regret was that I could not accompany him, but this was impossible at the time. I assisted him in every way possible in the organization of his safari and in equipping and provisioning it.

"He has not been gone a sufficient length of time to accomplish any considerable investigation and return to the mission, but recently a few of the members of his safari were reported to me as having returned to their villages. When I sought to interview them they avoided me, but rumors reached me that convinced me that all was not well with my son. I therefore determined to organize a relief expedition, but in all my district I could find only these few men who dared accompany me to the Wiramwazi Mountains, which, their legends assure them, are inhabited by malign spirits—for, as you know, they consider The Lost Tribe of the Wiramwazi to be a band of bloodthirsty ghosts. It became evident to me that the deserters of Erich's safari had spread terror through the district.

"Under the circumstances I was compelled to look elsewhere for help and naturally I turned, in my perplexity, to Tarzan, Lord of the Jungle. . . . Now you know why I am here."

"I will help you, Doctor," said Tarzan, after the other had concluded.

"Good!" exclaimed von Harben; "but I knew that you would. You have about twenty men here, I should judge, and I have about fourteen. My men can act as carriers, while yours, who are acknowledged to be the finest fighting men in Africa, can serve as askaris. With you to guide us we can soon pick up the trail and with such a force, small though it be, there is no country that we cannot penetrate."

Tarzan shook his head. "No, Doctor," he said, "I shall go alone. That is always my way. Alone I may travel much more rapidly and when I am alone the jungle holds no secrets from me—I shall be able to obtain more information along the way than would be possible were I accompanied by others. You know the jungle people consider me as one of themselves. They do not run away from me as they would from you and other men."

"You know best," said von Harben. "I should like to accompany you. I should like to feel that I am doing my share, but if you say no I can only abide by your decision."

"Return to your mission, Doctor, and wait there until you hear from me."

"And in the morning you leave for the Wiramwazi Mountains?" asked von Harben.

"I leave at once," said the ape-man.

"But it is already dark," objected von Harben.

"There is a full moon and I wish to take advantage of it," explained the other. "I can lie up in the heat of the day for what rest I need." He turned and called Muviro to him. "Return home with my warriors, Muviro," he instructed, "and hold every fighting man of the Waziri in readiness in the event that I find it necessary to send for you."

"Yes, Bwana," replied Muviro; "and how long shall we wait for a message before we set out for the Wiramwazi Mountains in search of you?"

"I shall take Nkima with me and if I need you I shall send him back to fetch and to guide you."

"Yes, Bwana," replied Muviro. "They will be in readiness—all the fighting men of the Waziri. Their weapons will be at hand by day and by night and fresh war-paint will be ready in every pot."

Tarzan swung his bow and his quiver of arrows across his back. Over his left shoulder and under his right arm lay the coils of his grass rope and at his hip dangled the hunting-knife of his long-dead sire. He picked up his short spear and stood for a moment with head up, sniffing the breeze. The firelight played upon his bronzed skin.

For a moment he stood thus, every sense alert. Then he called to Nkima in the tongue of the ape folk and as the little monkey scampered toward him, Tarzan of the Apes turned without a word of farewell and moved silently off into the jungle, his lithe carriage, his noiseless tread, his majestic mien suggesting to the mind of von Harben a personification of another mighty jungle animal, Numa the lion, king of beasts.

2

ERICH VON HARBEN stepped from his tent upon the slopes of the Wiramwazi Mountains to look upon a deserted camp.

When he had first awakened, the unusual quiet of his surroundings had aroused within him a presentiment of ill, which was augmented when repeated calls for his bodyservant, Gabula, elicited no response.

For weeks, as the safari had been approaching the precincts of the feared Wiramwazi, his men had been deserting by twos and threes until the preceding evening when they had made this camp well upon the mountain slopes only a terrified remnant of the original safari had remained with him. Now even these, overcome during the night by the terrors of ignorance and superstition, had permitted fear to supplant loyalty and had fled from the impending and invisible terrors of this frowning range, leaving their master alone with the bloodthirsty spirits of the dead.

A hasty survey of the camp site revealed that the men had stripped von Harben of everything. All of his supplies were gone and his gun carriers had decamped with his rifles and all of his ammunition, with the exception of a single Luger pistol and its belt of ammunition that had been in the tent with him.

Erich von Harben had had sufficient experience with these natives to understand fairly well the mental processes based upon their deep-rooted superstition that had led them to this seemingly inhuman and disloyal act and so he did not place so much blame upon them as might another less familiar with them.

While they had known their destination when they embarked upon the undertaking, their courage had been high in direct proportion to the great distance that they had been from the Wiramwazi, but in proportion as the distance lessened with each day's march their courage had lessened until now upon the very threshold of horrors beyond the ken of human minds the last vestige of self-control had deserted them and they had fled precipitately.

That they had taken his provisions, his rifles and his ammunition might have seemed the depth of baseness had von Harben not realized the sincerity of their belief that there could be no possible hope for him and that his immediate death was a foregone conclusion.

He knew that they had reasoned that under the circumstances it would be a waste of food to leave it behind for a man who was already as good as dead when they would need it for their return journey to their villages, and likewise, as the weapons of mortal man could avail nothing against the ghosts of Wiramwazi, it would have been a needless extravagance to have surrendered fine rifles and quantities of ammunition that von Harben could not use against his enemies of the spirit world.

Von Harben stood for some time looking down the mountain slope toward the forest, somewhere in the depths of which his men were hastening toward their own country. That he might overtake them was a possibility, but by no means a certainty, and if he did not he would be no better off alone in the jungle than he would be on the slopes of the Wiramwazi.

He faced about and looked up toward the rugged heights above him. He had come a long way to reach his goal, which now lay somewhere just beyond that serrated skyline, and he was of no mind to turn back now in defeat. A day or a week in these rugged mountains might reveal the secret of The Lost Tribe of legend, and surely a month would be sufficient to determine beyond a reasonable doubt that the story had no basis in fact, for von Harben believed that in a month he could fairly well explore such portions of the range as might naturally lend themselves to human habitation, where he hoped at best to find relics of the fabled tribe in the form of ruins or burial mounds. For to a man of von Harben's training and intelligence there could be no thought that The Lost Tribe of legend, if it had ever existed, could be anything more than a vague memory surrounding a few moldy artifacts and some crumbling bones.

It did not take the young man long to reach a decision and presently he turned back to his tent and, entering it, packed a few necessities that had been left to him in a light haversack, strapped his ammunition belt about him,

11

and stepped forth once more to turn his face upward toward the mystery of the Wiramwazi.

In addition to his Luger, von Harben carried a hunting-knife and with this he presently cut a stout staff from one of the small trees that grew sparsely upon the mountainside against the time when he might find an alpenstock indispensable.

A mountain rill furnished him pure, cold water to quench his thirst, and he carried his pistol cocked, hoping that he might bag some small game to satisfy his hunger. Nor had he gone far before a hare broke cover, and as it rolled over to the crack of the Luger, von Harben gave thanks that he had devoted much time to perfecting himself in the use of small arms.

On the spot he built a fire and grilled the hare, after which he lit his pipe and lay at ease while he smoked and planned. His was not a temperament to be depressed or discouraged by seeming reverses, and he was determined not to be hurried by excitement, but to conserve his strength at all times during the strenuous days that he felt must lie ahead of him.

All day he climbed, choosing the long way when it seemed safer, exercising all the lore of mountain-climbing that he had accumulated, and resting often. Night overtook him well up toward the summit of the highest ridge that had been visible from the base of the range. What lay behind, he could not even guess, but experience suggested that he would find other ridges and frowning peaks before him.

He had brought a blanket with him from the last camp and in this he rolled up on the ground. From below there came the noises of the jungle subdued by distance—the yapping of jackals and faintly from afar the roaring of a lion.

Toward morning he was awakened by the scream of a leopard, not from the jungle far below, but somewhere upon the mountain slopes near by. He knew that this savage night prowler constituted a real menace, perhaps the greatest he would have to face, and he regretted the loss of his heavy rifle.

He was not afraid, for he knew that after all there was little likelihood that the leopard was hunting him or that it would attack him, but there was always that chance and so to guard against it he started a fire of dry wood that he had gathered for the purpose the night before. He found the warmth of the blaze welcome, for the night had grown cold, and he sat for some time warming himself.

Once he thought he heard an animal moving in the

darkness beyond the range of the firelight, but he saw no shining eyes and the sound was not repeated. And then he must have slept, for the next thing that he knew it was daylight and only embers remained to mark where the beast fire had blazed.

Cold and without breakfast, von Harben continued the ascent from his cheerless camp, his eyes, under the constant urging of his stomach, always alert for food. The terrain offered few obstacles to an experienced mountain climber, and he even forgot his hunger in the thrill of expectancy with which he anticipated the possibilities hidden by the ridge whose summit now lay but a short distance ahead of him.

It is the summit of the next ridge that ever lures the explorer onward. What new sights lie just beyond? What mysteries will its achievement unveil to the eager eyes of the adventurer? Judgment and experience joined forces to assure him that when his eyes surmounted the ridge ahead they would be rewarded with nothing more startling than another similar ridge to be negotiated; yet there was always that other hope hanging like a shining beacon just below the next horizon, above which the rays of its hidden light served to illuminate the figments of his desire, and his imagination transformed the figments into realities.

Von Haben, sane and phlegmatic as he was, was now keyed to the highest pitch of excitement as he at last scaled the final barrier and stood upon the crest of the ridge. Before him stretched a rolling plateau, dotted with stunted wind-swept trees, and in the distance lay the next ridge that he had anticipated, but indistinct and impurpled by the haze of distance. What lay between him and those far hills? His pulse quickened at the thought of the possibilities for exploration and discovery that lay before him, for the terrain that he looked upon was entirely different from what he had anticipated. No lofty peaks were visible except in the far distance, and between him and them there must lie intriguing ravines and valleys—virgin fields at the feet of the explorer.

Eagerly, entirely forgetful of his hunger or his solitude, von Harben moved northward across the plateau. The land was gently rolling, rock-strewn, sterile, and uninteresting, and when he had covered a mile of it he commenced to have misgivings, for if it continued on without change to the dim hills in the distance, as it now seemed was quite likely the case, it could offer him neither interest nor sustenance.

As these thoughts were commencing to oppress him, he became suddenly conscious of a vague change in the appearance of the terrain ahead. It was only an impression of unreality. The hills far away before him seemed to rise out of a great void, and it was as though between him and them there existed nothing. He might have been looking across an inland sea to distant, hazy shores—a waterless sea, for nowhere was there any suggestion of water—and then suddenly he came to a halt, startled, amazed. The rolling plateau ceased abruptly at his feet, and below him, stretching far to the distant hills, lay a great abyss—a mighty canyon similar to that which has made the gorge of the Colorado world-famous.

But here there was a marked difference. There were indications of erosion. The grim walls were scarred and waterworn. Towers and turrets and minarets, carved from the native granite, pointed upward from below, but they clung close to the canyon's wall, and just beyond them he could see the broad expanse of the floor of the canyon, which from his great height above it appeared as level as a billiard table. The scene held him in a hypnosis of wonderment and admiration as, at first swiftly and then slowly, his eyes encompassed the whole astounding scene.

Perhaps a mile below him lay the floor of the sunken canyon, the further wall of which he could but vaguely estimate to be somewhere between fifteen and twenty miles to the north, and this he realized was the lesser dimension of the canyon. Upon his right, to the east, and upon his left, to the west, he could see that the canyon extended to considerable distances—just how far he could not guess. He thought that to the east he could trace the wall that hemmed it upon that side, but from where he stood the entire extent of the canyon to the west was not visible, yet he knew that the floor that was visible to him must stretch fully twenty-five or thirty miles from east to west. Almost below him was a large lake or marsh that seemed to occupy the greater part of the east end of the canyon. He could see lanes of water winding through what appeared to be great growths of reeds and, nearer the northern shore, a large island. Three streams, winding ribbons far below, emptied into the lake, and in the far distance was another ribbon that might be a road. To the west the canyon was heavily wooded, and between the forest and the lake he saw moving figures of what he thought to be grazing game.

The sight below him aroused the enthusiasm of the explorer to its highest pitch. Here, doubtless, lay the secret of The Lost Tribe of the Wiramwazi and how well Nature had guarded this secret with stupendous barrier cliffs, aided by the supersitions of the ignorant inhabitants of the outer slopes, was now easily understandable.

As far as he could see, the cliffs seemed sheer and impossible of descent, and yet he knew that he must find a way—that he would find a way down into that valley of enchantment.

Moving slowly along the rim he sought some foothold, however slight, where Nature had lowered her guard, but it was almost night and he had covered but a short distance before he found even a suggestion of hope that the canyon was hemmed at any point by other than unbroken cliffs, whose perpendicular faces rose at their lowest point fully a thousand feet above any possible foothold for a human being.

The sun had already set when he discovered a narrow fissure in the granite wall. Crumbled fragments of the mother rock had fallen into and partially filled it so that near the surface, at least, it offered a means of descent below the level of the cliff top, but in the gathering darkness he could not determine how far downward this rough and precarious pathway led.

He could see that below him the cliffs rose in terraced battlements to within a thousand feet of where he stood, and if the narrow fissure extended to the next terrace below him, he felt that the obstacles thereafter would present fewer difficulties than those that had baffled him up to the present time—for while he would still have some four thousand feet to descend, the formation of the cliffs was much more broken at the foot of the first sheer drop and consequently might be expected to offer some avenues of descent of which an experienced mountain climber could take advantage.

Hungry and cold, he sat beneath the descending night, gazing down into the blackening void below. Presently, as the darkness deepened, he saw a light twinkling far below and then another and another and with each his excitement rose, for he knew that they marked the presence of man. In many places upon the marsh-like lake he saw the fires twinkling, and at a point which he took to mark the site of the island there were many lights.

What sort of men were they who tended these fires? Would he find them friendly or hostile? Were they but another tribe of Africans, or could it be that the old legend was based upon truth and that far below him white men of The Lost Tribe cooked their evening meals above those tantalizing fires of mystery?

What was that? Von Harben strained his ears to catch the faint suggestion of a sound that arose out of the shadowy abyss below—a faint, thin sound that barely reached his ears, but he was sure that he could not be mistaken—the sound was the voices of men.

15

And now from out of the valley came the scream of a beast and again a roar that rumbled upward like distant thunder. To the music of these sounds, von Harben finally succumbed to exhaustion; sleep for the moment offering him relief from cold and hunger.

When morning came he gathered wood from the stunted trees near by and built a fire to warm himself. He had no food, nor all the previous day since he had reached the summit had he seen any sign of a living creature other than the game a mile beneath him on the verdant meadows of the canyon bottom.

He knew that he must have food and have it soon and food lay but a mile away in one direction. If he sought to circle the canyon in search of an easier avenue of descent, he knew that he might not find one in the hundred miles or more that he must travel. Of course he might turn back. He was sure that he could reach the base of the outer slopes of the Wiramwazi, where he knew that game might be found before exhaustion overcame him, but he had no mind to turn back and the thought of failure was only a vague suggestion that scarcely ever rose above the threshold of his conscious mind.

Having warmed himself before the fire, he turned to examine the fissure by the full light of day. As he stood upon its brink he could see that it extended downward for several hundred feet, but there it disappeared. However, he was by no means sure that it ended, since it was not a vertical cleft, but tilted slightly from the perpendicular.

From where he stood he could see that there were places in the fissure where descent would be just possible, though it might be very difficult to reascend. He knew, therefore, that should he reach the bottom of the fissure and find that further descent was impossible he would be caught in a trap from which there might be no escape.

Although he felt as fit and strong as ever, he realized perfectly that the contrary was the fact and that his strength must be ebbing and that it would continue to ebb still more rapidly the longer that he was forced to expend it in arduous efforts to descend the cliff and without any possibility of rebuilding it with food.

Even to Erich von Harben, young, self-confident and enthusiastic, his next step seemed little better than suicidal. To another the mere idea of attempting the descent of these towering cliffs would have seemed madness, but in other mountains von Harben had always found a way, and with this thin thread upon which to hang his hopes he faced the descent into the unknown. Now he was just about to lower himself over the edge of the fissure when he heard the sounds of footsteps behind him. Wheeling quickly, he drew his Luger.

3

LITTLE NKIMA came racing through the tree tops, jabbering excitedly, and dropped to the knee of Tarzan of the Apes where the latter lay stretched upon the great branch of a jungle giant, his back against the rough bole, where he was lying up after making a kill and feeding.

"Gomangani! Gomangani!" shrilled Nkima. "They come! They come!"

"Peace," said Tarzan. "You are a greater nuisance than all the Gomangani in the jungle."

"They will kill little Nkima," cried the monkey. "They are strange Gomangani, and there are no Tarmangani among them."

"Nkima thinks everything wants to kill him," said Tarzan, "and yet he has lived many years and is not dead yet."

"Sabor and Shetta and Numa, the Gomangani, had Histah the snake like to eat poor little Nkima," wailed the monkey. "That is why he is afraid."

"Do not fear, Nkima," said the ape-man. "Tarzan will let no one hurt you."

"Go and see the Gomangani," urged Nkima. "Go and kill them. Nkima does not like the Gomangani."

Tarzan arose leisurely. "I go," he said. "Nkima may come or he may hide in the upper terraces."

"Nkima is not afraid," blustered the little monkey. "He will go and fight the Gomangani with Tarzan of the Apes," and he leaped to the back of the ape-man and clung there with his arms about the bronzed throat, from which point of vantage he peered fearfully ahead, first over the top of one broad shoulder and then over the top of the other.

Tarzan swung swiftly and quietly through the trees toward a point where Nkima had discovered the Gomangani, and presently he saw below him some score of natives straggling along the jungle trail. A few of them were armed with rifles and all carried packs of various sizes—such packs as Tarzan knew must belong to the equipment of a white man.

The Lord of the Jungle hailed them and, startled, the men halted, looking up fearfully.

"I am Tarzan of the Apes. Do not be afraid," Tarzan reassured them, and simultaneously he dropped lightly to the trail among them, but as he did so Nkima leaped frantically from his shoulders and scampered swiftly to a high branch far above, where he sat chattering and scolding, entirely forgetful of his vain boasting of a few moments before.

"Where is your master?" demanded Tarzan.

The Africans looked sullenly at the ground, but did not reply.

"Where is the Bwana, von Harben?" Tarzan insisted.

A tall man standing near fidgeted uneasily. "He is dead," he mumbled.

"How did he die?" asked Tarzan.

Again the man hesitated before replying. "A bull elephant that he had wounded killed him," he said at last.

"Where is his body?"

"We could not find it."

"Then how do you know that he was killed by a bull elephant?" demanded the ape-man.

"We do not know," another spoke up. "He went away from camp and did not return."

"There was an elephant about and we thought that it had killed him," said the tall man.

"You are not speaking true words," said Tarzan.

"I shall tell you the truth," said a third. "Our Bwana ascended the slopes of the Wiramwazi and the spirits of the dead being angry seized him and carried him away."

"I shall tell you the truth," said Tarzan. "You have deserted your master and run away, leaving him alone in the forest."

"We were afraid," the man replied. "We warned him not to ascend the slopes of the Wiramwazi. We begged him to turn back. He would not listen to us, and the spirits of the dead carried him away."

"How long ago was that?" asked the ape-man.

"Six, seven, perhaps ten marchings. I do not remember."

"Where was he when you last saw him?"

As accurately as they could the men described the location of their last camp upon the slopes of the Wiramwazi.

"Go your way back to your own villages in the Urambi country. I shall know where to find you if I want you. If your Bwana is dead, you shall be punished," and swinging into the branches of the lower terrace, Tarzan disappeared from the sight of the unhappy natives in the direction of

18

the Wiramwazi, while Nkima, screaming shrilly, raced through the trees to overtake him.

From his conversation with the deserting members of von Harben's safari, Tarzan was convinced that the young man had been traitorously abandoned and that in all likelihood he was making his way alone back upon the trail of the deserters.

Not knowing Erich von Harben, Tarzan could not have guessed that the young man would push on alone into the unknown and forbidding depths of the Wiramwazi, but assumed on the contrary that he would adopt the more prudent alternative and seek to overtake his men as rapidly as possible. Believing this, the ape-man followed back along the trail of the safari, expecting momentarily to meet von Harben.

This plan greatly reduced his speed, but even so he traveled with so much greater rapidity than the natives that he came to the slopes of the Wiramwazi upon the third day after he had interviewed the remnants of von Harben's safari.

It was with great difficulty that he finally located the point at which von Harben had been abandoned by his men, as a heavy rain and wind-storm had obliterated the trail, but at last he stumbled upon the tent, which had blown down, but nowhere could he see any signs of von Harben's trail.

Not having come upon any signs of the white man in the jungle or any indication that he had followed his fleeing safari, Tarzan was forced to the conclusion that if von Harben was not indeed dead he must have faced the dangers of the unknown alone and now be either dead or alive somewhere within the mysterious fastnesses of the Wiramwazi.

"Nkima," said the ape-man, "the Tarmangani have a saying that when it is futile to search for a thing, it is like hunting for a needle in a haystack. Do you believe, Nkima, that in this great mountain range we shall find our needle?"

"Let us go home," said Nkima, "where it is warm. Here the wind blows and up there it is colder. It is no place for little Manu, the monkey."

"Nevertheless, Nkima, there is where we are going."

The monkey looked up toward the frowning heights above. "Little Nkima is afraid," he said. "It is in such places that Sheeta, the panther, lairs."

Ascending diagonally and in a westerly direction in the hope of crossing von Harben's trail, Tarzan moved constantly in the opposite direction from that taken by the man he sought. It was his intention, however, when he reached the summit, if he had in the meantime found no trace of von Harben, to turn directly eastward and search at a higher altitude in the opposite direction. As he proceeded, the slope became steeper and more rugged until at one point near the western end of the mountain mass he encountered an almost perpendicular barrier high up on the mountainside along the base of which he picked his precarious way among loose bowlders that had fallen from above. Underbrush and stunted trees extended at different points from the forest below quite up to the base of the vertical escarpment.

So engrossed was the ape-man in the dangerous business of picking his way along the mountainside that he gave little heed to anything beyond the necessities of the trail and his constant search for the spoor of von Harben, and so he did not see the little group of warriors that were gazing up at him from the shelter of a clump of trees far down the slope, nor did Nkima, usually as alert as his master, have eyes or ears for anything beyond the immediate exigencies of the trail. Nkima was unhappy. The wind blew and Nkima did not like the wind. All about him he smelled the spoor of Sheeta, the panther, while he considered the paucity and stunted nature of the few trees along the way that his master had chosen. From time to time he noted, with sinking heart, ledges just above them from which Sheeta might spring down upon them; and the way was a way of terror for little Nkima.

Now they had come to a particularly precarious point upon the mountainside. A sheer cliff rose above them on their right and at their left the mountainside fell away so steeply that as Tarzan advanced his body was pressed closely against the granite face of the cliff as he sought a foothold upon the ledge of loose rubble. Just ahead of them the cliff shouldered out boldly against the distant skies. Perhaps beyond that clear-cut corner the going might be better. If it should develop that it was worse, Tarzan realized that he must turn back.

At the turn where the footing was narrowest a stone gave beneath Tarzan's foot, throwing him off his balance for an instant and at that same instant Nkima, thinking that Tarzan was falling, shrieked and leaped from his shoulder, giving the ape-man's body just the impetus that was required to overbalance it entirely.

The mountainside below was steep, though not perpendicular, and if Nkima had not pushed the ape-man outward he doubtless would have slid but a short distance before being able to stay his fall, but as it was he lunged headforemost down the embankment, rolling and tumbling for a short distance over the loose rock until his body was brought to a stop by one of the many stunted trees that clung tenaciously to the wind-swept slope.

Terrified, Nkima scampered to his master's side. He screamed and chattered in his ear and pulled and tugged upon him in an effort to raise him, but the ape-man lay motionless, a tiny stream of blood trickling from a cut on his temple into his shock of black hair.

As Nkima mourned, the warriors, who had been watching them from below, clambered quickly up the mountainside toward him and his helpless master.

4

As Erich von Harben turned to face the thing that he had heard approaching behind him, he saw a Negro armed with a rifle coming toward him.

"Gabula!" exclaimed the white man, lowering his weapon. "What are you doing here?"

"Bwana," said the warrior, "I could not desert you. I could not leave you to die alone at the hands of the spirits that dwell upon these mountains."

Von Harben eyed him incredulously. "But if you believe that, Gabula, are you not afraid that they will kill you, too?"

"I expect to die, Bwana," replied Gabula. "I cannot understand why you were not killed the first night or the second night. We shall both surely be killed tonight."

"And yet you followed me! Why?"

"You have been kind to me, Bwana," replied the man. "Your father has been kind to me. When the others talked they filled me with fear and when they ran away I went with them, but I have come back. There was nothing else that I could do, was there?"

"No, Gabula. For you or for me there would have been nothing else to do, as we see such things, but as the others saw them they found another thing to do and they did it."

"Gabula is not as the others," said the man, proudly. "Gabula is a Batoro."

"Gabula is a brave warrior," said von Harben. "I do not believe in spirits and so there was no reason why I should be afraid, but you and all your people do believe in them and so it was a very brave thing for you to come back, but I shall not hold you. You may return, Gabula, with the others."

"Yes?" Gabula exclaimed eagerly. "The Bwana is going

back? That will be good. Gabula will go back with him."

"No, I am going down into that canyon," said von Harben, pointing over the rim.

Gabula looked down, surprise and wonder reflected by his wide eyes and parted lips.

"But, Bwana, even if a human being could find a way down these steep cliffs, where there is no place for either hand or foot, he would surely be killed the moment he reached the bottom, for this indeed must be the Land of The Lost Tribe where the spirits of the dead live in the heart of the Wiramwazi."

"You do not need to come with me, Gabula," said von Harben. "Go back to your people."

"How are you going to get down there?" demanded the Negro.

"I do not know just how, or where, or when. Now I am going to descend as far along this fissure as I can go. Perhaps I shall find my way down here, perhaps not."

"But suppose there is no foothold beyond the fissure?" asked Gabula.

"I shall have to find footing."

Gabula shook his head. "And if you reach the bottom, Bwana, and you are right about the spirits and there are none or they do not kill you, how will you get out again?"

Von Harben shrugged his shoulders and smiled. Then he extended his hand. "Goodby, Gabula," he said. "You are a brave man."

Gabula did not take the offered hand of his master. "I am going with you," he said, simply.

"Even though you realize that should we reach the bottom alive we may never be able to return?"

"Yes."

"I cannot understand you, Gabula. You are afraid and I know that you wish to return to the village of your people. Then why do you insist on coming with me when I give you leave to return home?"

"I have sworn to serve you, Bwana, and I am a Batoro," replied Gabula.

"And I can only thank the Lord that you are a Batoro," said von Harben, "for the Lord knows that I shall need help before I reach the bottom of this canyon, and we must reach it, Gabula, unless we are content to die by starvation."

"I have brought food," said Gabula. "I knew that you might be hungry and I brought some of the food that you like," and, unrolling the small pack that he carried, he displayed several bars of chocolate and a few packages of concentrated food that von Harben had included among his supplies in the event of an emergency.

To the famished von Harben, the food was like manna to the Israelites, and he lost no time in taking advantage of Gabula's thoughtfulness. The sharp edge of his hunger removed, von Harben experienced a feeling of renewed strength and hopefulness, and it was with a light heart and a buoyant optimism that he commenced the descent into the canyon.

Gabula's ancestry, stretching back through countless generations of jungle-dwelling people, left him appalled as he contemplated the frightful abyss into which his master was leading him, but so deeply had he involved himself by his protestations of loyalty and tribal pride that he followed von Harben with no outward show of the real terror that was consuming him.

The descent through the fissure was less difficult than it had appeared from above. The tumbled rocks that had partially filled it gave more than sufficient footing and in only a few places was assistance required, and it was at these times that von Harben realized how fortunate for him had been Gabula's return.

When at last they reached the bottom of the cleft they found themselves, at its outer opening, flush with the face of the cliff and several hundred feet below the rim. This was the point beyond which von Harben had been unable to see and which he had been approaching with deep anxiety, since there was every likelihood that the conditions here might put a period to their further descent along this route.

Creeping over the loose rubble in the bottom of the fissure to its outer edge, von Harben discovered a sheer drop of a hundred feet to the level of the next terrace and his heart sank. To return the way they had come was, he feared, a feat beyond their strength and ingenuity, for there had been places down which one had lowered the other only with the greatest difficulty, which would be practically unscalable on the return journey.

It being impossible to ascend and as starvation surely faced them where they were, there was but one alternative. Von Harben lay upon his belly, his eyes at the outer edge of the fissure, and, instructing Gabula to hold tightly to his ankles, he wormed himself forward until he could scan the entire face of the cliff below him to the level of the next terrace.

A few feet from the level on which he lay he saw that the fissure lay open again to the base of the cliff, its stoppage at the point where they were having been caused by a large fragment of rock that had wedged securely between the sides of the fissure, entirely choking it at this point.

The fissure, which had narrowed considerably since they had entered it at the summit, was not more than two or three feet wide directly beneath the rock on which he lay and extended with little variation at this width the remaining hundred feet to the comparatively level ground below.

If he and Gabula could but get into this crevice he knew that they could easily brace themselves against its sides in such a way as to descend safely the remaining distance, but how with the means at hand were they to climb over the edge of the rock that blocked the fissure and crawl back into the fissure again several feet farther down?

Von Harben lowered his crude alpenstock over the edge of the rock fragment. When he extended his arms at full length the tip of the rod fell considerably below the bottom of the rock on which he lay. A man hanging at the end of the alpenstock might conceivably swing into the fissure, but it would necessitate a feat of acrobatics far beyond the powers of either himself or Gabula.

A rope would have solved their problem, but they had no rope. With a sigh, von Harben drew back when his examination of the fissure convinced him that he must find another way, but he was totally at a loss to imagine in what direction to look for a solution.

Gabula crouched back in the fissure, terrified by the anticipation of what von Harben's attempted exploration had suggested. The very thought of even looking out over the edge of that rock beyond the face of the cliff left Gabula cold and half paralyzed, while the thought that he might have to follow von Harben bodily over the edge threw the Negro into a fit of trembling; yet had von Harben gone over the edge Gabula would have followed him.

The white man sat for a long time buried in thought. Time and again his eyes examined every detail of the formation of the fissure within the range of his vision. Again and again they returned to the huge fragment upon which they sat, which was securely wedged between the fissure's sides. With this out of the way he felt that they could make unimpeded progress to the next terrace, but he knew that nothing short of a charge of dynamite could budge the heavy granite slab. Directly behind it were loose fragments of various sizes, and as his eyes returned to them once again he was struck with the possibility that they suggested.

"Come, Gabula," he said. "Help me throw out some of these rocks. This seems to be our only possible hope of escaping from the trap that I have got us into."

"Yes, Bwana," replied Gabula, and fell to work beside von Harben, though he could not understand why they should be picking up these stones, some of which were very heavy, and pushing them out over the edge of the flat fragment that clogged the fissure.

He heard them crash heavily where they struck the rocks below and this interested and fascinated him to such an extent that he worked feverishly to loosen the larger blocks of stone for the added pleasure he derived from hearing the loud noise that they made when they struck.

"It begins to look," said von Harben, after a few minutes, "as though we may be going to succeed, unless by removing these rocks here we cause some of those above to slide down and thus loosen the whole mass above us—in which event, Gabula, the mystery of The Lost Tribe will cease to interest us longer."

"Yes, Bwana," said Gabula, and lifting an unusually large rock he started to roll it toward the edge of the fissure. "Look! Look, Bwana!" he exclaimed, pointing at the place where the rock had lain.

Von Harben looked and saw an opening about the size of a man's head extending into the fissure beneath them.

"Thank Nsenene, the grasshopper, Gabula," cried the white man, "if that is the totem of your clan—for here indeed is a way to salvation."

Hurriedly the two men set to work to enlarge the hole by throwing out other fragments that had long been wedged in together to close the fissure at this point, and as the fragments clattered down upon the rocks below, a tall, straight warrior standing in the bow of a dugout upon the marshy lake far below looked up and called the attention of his comrades.

They could plainly hear the reverberations of the falling fragments as they struck the rocks at the foot of the fissure and, keen-eyed, they could see many of the larger pieces that von Harben and Gabula tossed downward.

"The great wall is falling," said the warrior.

"A few pebbles," said another. "It is nothing."

"Such things do not happen except after rains," said the first speaker. "It is thus that it is prophesied that the great wall will fall."

"Perhaps it is a demon who lives in the great rift in the wall," said another. "Let us hasten and tell the masters."

"Let us wait and watch," said the first speaker, "until we have something to tell them. If we went and told them that a few rocks had fallen from the great wall they would only laugh at us."

Von Harben and Gabula had increased the size of the opening until it was large enough to permit the passage of a man's body. Through it the white man could see the rough sides of the fissure extending to the level of the next terrace and knew that the next stage of the descent was already as good as an accomplished fact.

"We shall descend one at a time, Gabula," said von Harben. "I shall go first, for I am accustomed to this sort of climbing. Watch carefully so that you may descend exactly as I do. It is easy and there is no danger. Be sure that you keep your back braced against one wall and your feet against the other. We shall lose some hide in the descent, for the walls are rough, but we shall get down safely enough if we take it slowly."

"Yes, Bwana. You go first," said Gabula. "If I see you do it then, perhaps, I can do it."

Von Harben lowered himself through the aperture, braced himself securely against the opposite walls of the fissure, and started slowly downward. A few minutes later Gabula saw his master standing safely at the bottom, and though his heart was in his mouth the Negro followed without hesitation, but when he stood at last beside von Harben he breathed such a loud sigh of relief that von Harben was forced to laugh aloud.

"It is the demon himself," said the warrior in the dugout, as von Harben had stepped from the fissure.

From where the dugout of the watchers floated, half concealed by lofty papyrus, the terrace at the base of the fissure was just visible. They saw von Harben emerge and a few moments later the figure of Gabula.

"Now, indeed," said one of the men, "we should hasten and tell the masters."

"No," said the first speaker. "Those two may be demons, but they look like men and we shall wait until we know what they are and why they are here before we go away."

For a thousand feet the descent from the base of the fissure was far from difficult, a rough slope leading in an easterly direction down toward the canyon bottom. During the descent their view of the lake and of the canyon was often completely shut off by masses of weather-worn granite around which they sometimes had difficulty in finding a way. As a rule the easiest descent lay between these towering fragments of the main body of the cliff, and at such times as the valley was hidden from them so were they hidden from the watchers on the lake.

A third of the way down the escarpment von Harben came to the verge of a narrow gorge, the bottom of which was densely banked with green, the foliage of trees growing luxuriantly, pointing unquestionably to the presence of water in abundance. Leading the way, von Harben descended into the gorge, at the bottom of which he found a spring from which a little stream trickled downward. Here they quenched their thirst and rested. Then, following the stream downward, they discovered no obstacles that might not be easily surmounted.

For a long time, hemmed in by the walls of the narrow gorge and their view further circumscribed by the forest-like growth along the banks of the stream, they had no sight of the lake or the canyon bottom, but, finally, when the gorge debouched upon the lower slopes von Harben halted in admiration of the landscape spread out before him. Directly below, another stream entered that along which they had descended, forming a little river that dropped steeply to what appeared to be vivid green meadow land through which it wound tortuously to the great swamp that extended out across the valley for perhaps ten miles.

So choked was the lake with some feathery-tipped acquatic plant that von Harben could only guess as to its extent, since the green of the water plant and the green of the surrounding meadows blended into one another, but here and there he saw signs of open water that appeared like winding lanes or passages leading in all directions throughout the marsh.

As von Harben and Gabula stood looking out across this (to them) new and mysterious world, the warriors in the dugout watched them attentively. The strangers were still so far away that the men were unable to identify them, but their leader assured them that these two were no demons.

"How do you know that they are not demons?" demanded one of these fellows.

"I can see that they are men," replied the other.

"Demons are very wise and very powerful," insisted the doubter. "They may take any form they choose. They might come as birds or animals or men."

"They are not fools," snapped the leader. "If a demon wished to descend the great wall he would not choose the hardest way. He would take the form of a bird and fly down."

The other scratched his head in perplexity, for he realized that here was an argument that would be difficult to controvert. For want of anything better to say, he suggested that they go at once and report the matter to their masters.

"No," said the leader. "We shall remain here until they come closer. It will be better for us if we can take them with us and show them to our masters."

The first few steps that von Harben took onto the grassy meadow land revealed the fact that it was a dangerous swamp from which only with the greatest difficulty were they able to extricate themselves.

Floundering back to solid ground, von Harben reconnoitered in search of some other avenue to more solid ground on the floor of the canyon, but he found that upon both sides of the river the swamp extended to the foot of the lowest terrace of the cliff, and low as these were in comparison to their lofty fellows towering far above them, they were still impassable barriers.

Possibly by reascending the gorge he might find an avenue to more solid ground toward the west, but as he had no actual assurance of this and as both he and Gabula were well-nigh exhausted from the physical strain of the descent, he preferred to find an easier way to the lake shore if it were possible.

He saw that while the river at this point was not swift, the current was rapid enough to suggest that the bottom might be sufficiently free from mud to make it possible for them to utilize it as an avenue to the lake, if it were not too deep.

To test the feasibility of the idea, he lowered himself into the water, holding to one end of his alpenstock, while Gabula seized the other. He found that the water came to his waist-line and that the bottom was firm and solid.

"Come on, Gabula. This is our way to the lake, I guess," he said.

As Gabula slipped into the water behind his master, the dugout containing the warriors pushed silently along the watery lane among the papyrus and with silent paddles was urged swiftly toward the mouth of the stream where it emptied into the lake.

As von Harben and Gabula descended the stream they found that the depth of the water did not greatly increase. Once or twice they stumbled into deeper holes and were forced to swim, but in other places the water shallowed until it was only to their knees, and thus they made their way down to the lake at the verge of which their view was shut off by clumps of papyrus rising twelve or fifteen feet above the surface of the water.

"It begins to look," said von Harben, "as though there is no solid ground along the shore line, but the roots of the papyus will hold us and if we can make our way to the west end of the lake I am sure that we shall find solid ground, for I am positive that I saw higher land there as we were descending the cliff."

Feeling their way cautiously along, they came at last to the first clump of papyrus and just as von Harben was about to clamber to the solid footing of the roots, a canoe shot from behind the mass of floating plants and the two men found themselves covered by the weapons of a boatload of warriors.

5

LUKEDI, the Bagego, carried a gourd of milk to a hut in the village of his people on the lower slopes at the west end of the Wiramwazi range.

Two stalwart spearmen stood guard at the doorway of the hut. "Nyuto has sent me with milk for the prisoner," said Lukedi. "Has his spirit returned to him?"

"Go in and see," directed one of the sentries.

Lukedi entered the hut and in the dim light saw the figure of a giant white man sitting upon the dirt floor gazing at him. The man's wrists were bound together behind his back and his ankles were secured with tough fiber strands.

"Here is food," said Lukedi, setting the gourd upon the ground near the prisoner.

"How can I eat with my hands tied behind my back?" demanded Tarzan. Lukedi scratched his head. "I do not know," he said. "Nyuto sent me with the food. He did not tell me to free your hands."

"Cut the bond," said Tarzan, "otherwise I cannot eat."

One of the spearmen entered the hut. "What is he saying?" he demanded.

"He says that he cannot eat unless his hands are freed," said Lukedi.

"Did Nyuto tell you to free his hands?" asked the spearman.

"No," said Lukedi.

The spearman shrugged his shoulders. "Leave the food then; that is all you were asked to do."

Lukedi turned to leave the hut. "Wait," said Tarzan. "Who is Nyuto?"

"He is chief of the Bagegos," said Lukedi.

"Go to him and tell him that I wish to see him. Tell him also that I cannot eat with my hands tied behind my back."

Lukedi was gone for half an hour. When he returned he brought an old, rusted slave chain and an ancient padlock.

"Nyuto says that we may chain him to the center pole and then cut the bonds that secure his hands," he said to the guard.

The three men entered the hut where Lukedi passed one end of the chain around the center pole, pulling it through a ring on the other end; the free end he then passed around Tarzan's neck, securing it there with the old slave padlock.

"Cut the bonds that hold his wrists," said Lukedi to one of the spearmen.

"Do it yourself," retorted the warrior. "Nyuto sent you to do it. He did not tell me to cut the bonds."

Lukedi hesitated. It was apparent that he was afraid.

"We will stand ready with our spears," said the guardsmen; "then he cannot harm you."

"I shall not harm him," said Tarzan. "Who are you anyway and who do you think I am?"

One of the guardsmen laughed. "He asked who we are as though he did not know!"

"We know who you are, all right," said the other warrior.

"I am Tarzan of the Apes," said the prisoner, "and I have no quarrel with the Bagegos."

The guardsman who had last spoken laughed again derisively. "That may be your name," he said. "You men of The Lost Tribe have strange names. Perhaps you have no quarrel with the Bagegos, but the Bagegos have a quarrel with you," and still laughing he left the hut followed by his companion, but the youth Lukedi remained, apparently fascinated by the prisoner at whom he stood staring as he might have stared at a deity.

Tarzan reached for the gourd and drank the milk it contained, and never once did Lukedi take his eyes from him.

"What is your name?" asked Tarzan.

"Lukedi," replied the youth.

"And you have never heard of Tarzan of the Apes?"

"No," replied the youth.

"Who do you think I am?" demanded the ape-man.

"We know that you belong to The Lost Tribe."

"But I thought the members of The Lost Tribe were supposed to be the spirits of the dead," said Tarzan.

"That we do not know," replied Lukedi. "Some think one way, some another; but you know, for you are one of them."

"I am not one of them," said Tarzan. "I come from a country farther south, but I have heard of the Bagegos and I have heard of The Lost Tribe."

"I do not believe you," said Lukedi.

"I speak the truth," said Tarzan.

Lukedi scratched his head. "Perhaps you do," he said. "You do not wear clothes like the members of The Lost Tribe, and the weapons that we found with you are different."

"You have seen members of The Lost Tribe?" asked Tarzan.

"Many times," replied Lukedi. "Once a year they come out of the bowels of the Wiramwazi and trade with us. They bring dried fish, snails, and iron and take in exchange salt, goats, and cows."

"If they come and trade with you peacefully, why do you make me a prisoner if you think I am one of them?" demanded Tarzan.

"Since the beginning we have been at war with the members of The Lost Tribe," replied Lukedi. "It is true that once a year we trade with them, but they are always our enemies."

"Why is that?" demanded the ape-man.

"Because at other times we cannot tell when they will come with many warriors and capture men, women, and children whom they take away with them into the Wiramwazi. None ever returns. We do not know what becomes of them. Perhaps they are eaten."

"What will your chief, Nyuto, do with me?" asked Tarzan.

"I do not know," said Lukedi. "They are discussing the question now. They all wish to put you to death, but there are some who believe that this would arouse the anger of the ghosts of all the dead Bagegos."

"Why should the ghosts of your dead wish to protect me?" demanded Tarzan.

"There are many who think that you members of The Lost Tribe are the ghosts of our dead," replied Lukedi.

"What do you think, Lukedi?" asked the ape-man.

"When I look at you I think that you are a man of flesh and blood the same as I, and so I think that perhaps you are telling me the truth when you say that you are not a member of The Lost Tribe, because I am sure that they are all ghosts."

"But when they come to trade with you and when they come to fight with you, can you not tell whether they are flesh and blood or not?"

"They are very powerful," said Lukedi. "They might come in the form of men in the flesh or they might come as snakes or lions. That is why we are not sure."

"And what do you think the council will decide to do with me?" asked Tarzan.

"I think that there is no doubt but that they will burn you alive, for thus both you and your spirit will be destroyed so that it cannot come back to haunt and annoy us."

"Have you seen or heard of another white man recently?" asked Tarzan.

"No," replied the youth. "Many years ago, before I can remember, two white men came who said that they were not members of The Lost Tribe, but we did not believe them

31

and they were killed. I must go now. I shall bring you more milk tomorrow."

After Lukedi had left, Tarzan commenced examining the chain, padlock, and the center pole of the hut in an effort to discover some means of escape. The hut was cylindrical and surmounted by a conical roof of grass. The side walls were of stakes set upright a few inches in the ground and fastened together at their tops and bottoms by creepers. The center pole was much heavier and was secured in position by rafters radiating from it to the top of the wall. The interior of the hut was plastered with mud, which had been thrown on with force and then smoothed with the palm of the hand. It was a common type with which Tarzan was familiar. He knew that there was a possibility that he might be able to raise the center pole and withdraw the chain from beneath it.

It would, of course, be difficult to accomplish this without attracting the attention of the guards, and there was a possibility that the center pole might be set sufficiently far in the ground to render it impossible for him to raise it. If he were given time he could excavate around the base of it, but inasmuch as one or the other of the sentries was continually poking his head into the hut to see that all was well, Tarzan saw little likelihood of his being able to free himself without being discovered.

As darkness settled upon the village Tarzan stretched himself upon the hard dirt floor of the hut and sought to sleep. For some time the noises of the village kept him awake, but at last he slept. How long thereafter it was that he was awakened he did not know. From childhood he had shared with the beasts, among whom he had been raised, the ability to awaken quickly and in full command of all his faculties. He did so now, immediately conscious that the noise that had aroused him came from an animal upon the roof of the hut. Whatever it was, it was working quietly, but to what end the ape-man could not imagine.

The acrid fumes of the village cook fires so filled the air that Tarzan was unable to catch the scent of the creature upon the roof. He carefully reviewed all the possible purposes for which an animal might be upon the thatched, dry-grass roof of the Bagego hut and through a process of elimination he could reach but one conclusion. That was that the thing upon the outside wished to come in and either it did not have brains enough to know that there was a doorway, or else it was too cunning to risk detection by attempting to pass the sentries.

But why should any animal wish to enter the hut? Tarzan lay upon his back, gazing up through the darkness in the direction of the roof above him as he tried to find an answer to his question. Presently, directly above his head, he saw a little ray of moonlight. Whatever it was upon the roof had made an opening that grew larger and larger as the creature quietly tore away the thatching. The aperture was being made close to the wall where the radiating rafters were farthest apart, but whether this was through intent or accident Tarzan could not guess. As the hole grew larger and he caught occasional glimpses of the thing silhouetted against the moonlit sky, a broad smile illuminated the face of the ape-man. Now he saw strong little fingers working at the twigs that were fastened laterally across the rafters to support the thatch and presently, after several of these had been removed, the opening was entirely closed by a furry little body that wriggled through and dropped to the floor close beside the prisoner.

"How did you find me, Nkima?" whispered Tarzan.

"Nkima followed," replied the little monkey. "All day he has been sitting in a high tree above the village watching this place and waiting for darkness. Why do you stay here, Tarzan of the Apes? Why do you not come away with little Nkima?"

"I am fastened here with a chain," said Tarzan. "I cannot come away."

"Nkima will go and bring Muviro and his warriors," said Nkima.

Of course he did not use these words at all, but what he said in the language of the apes conveyed the same meaning to Tarzan. Black apes carrying sharp, long sticks was the expression that he used to describe the Waziri warriors, and the name for Muviro was one of his own coining, but he and Tarzan understood one another.

"No," said Tarzan. "If I am going to need Muviro, he could not get here in time now to be of any help to me. Go back into the forest, Nkima, and wait for me. Perhaps I shall join you very soon."

Nkima scolded, for he did not want to go away. He was afraid alone in this strange forest; in fact, Nkima's life had been one long complex of terror, relieved only by those occasions when he could snuggle in the lap of his master, safe within the solid walls of Tarzan's bungalow. One of the sentries heard the voices within the hut and crawled part way in.

"There," said Tarzan to Nkima, "you see what you have done. Now you had better do as Tarzan tells you and get out of here and into the forest before they catch you and eat you."

"Who are you talking to?" demanded the sentry. He heard

33

a scampering in the darkness and at the same instant he caught sight of the hole in the roof and almost simultaneously he saw something dark go through it and disappear. "What was that?" he demanded, nervously.

"That," said Tarzan, "was the ghost of your grandfather. He came to tell me that you and your wives and all your children would take sick and die if anything happens to me. He also brought the same message for Nyuto."

The sentry trembled. "Call him back," he begged, "and tell him that I had nothing to do with it. It is not I, but Nyuto, the chief, who is going to kill you."

"I cannot call him back," said Tarzan, "and so you had better tell Nyuto not to kill me."

"I cannot see Nyuto until morning," wailed the sentry. "Perhaps then it will be too late."

"No," said Tarzan. "The ghost of your grandfather will not do anything until tomorrow."

Terrified, the sentry returned to his post where Tarzan heard him fearfully and excitedly discussing the matter with his companion until the ape-man finally dropped off to sleep again.

It was late the following morning before anyone entered the hut in which Tarzan was confined. Then came Lukedi with another gourd of milk. He was very much excited.

"Is what Ogonyo says true?" he demanded.

"Who is Ogonyo?" asked Tarzan.

"He was one of the warriors who stood guard here last night, and he has told Nyuto and all the village that he heard the ghost of his grandfather talking with you and that the ghost said that he would kill everyone in the village if you were harmed, and now everyone is afraid."

"And Nyuto?" asked Tarzan.

"Nyuto is not afraid of anything," said Lukedi.

"Not even of ghosts of grandfathers?" asked Tarzan.

"No. He alone of all the Bagegos is not afraid of the men of The Lost Tribe, and now he is very angry at you because you have frightened his people and this evening you are to be burned. Look!" And Lukedi pointed to the low doorway of the hut. "From here you can see them placing the stake to which you are to be bound, and the boys are in the forest gathering fagots."

Tarzan pointed toward the hole in the roof. "There," he said, "is the hole made by the ghost of Ogonyo's grandfather. Fetch Nyuto and let him see. Then, perhaps, he will believe."

"It will make no difference," said Lukedi. "If he saw a thousand ghosts with his own eyes, he would not be afraid.

He is very brave, but he is also very stubborn and a fool. Now we shall all die."

"Unquestionably," said Tarzan.

"Can you not save me?" asked Lukedi.

"If you will help me to escape, I promise you that the ghosts shall not harm you."

"Oh, if I could but do it," said Lukedi, as he passed the gourd of milk to the ape-man.

"You bring me nothing but milk," said Tarzan. "Why is that?"

"In this village we belong to the Buliso clan and, therefore, we may not drink the milk nor eat the flesh of Timba, the black cow, so when we have guests or prisoners we save this food for them."

Tarzan was glad that the totem of the Buliso clan was a cow instead of a grasshopper, or rainwater from the roofs of houses or one of the hundreds of other objects that are venerated by different clans, for while Tarzan's early training had not placed grasshoppers beyond the pale as food for men, he much preferred the milk of Timba.

"I wish that Nyuto would see me and talk with me," said Tarzan of the Apes. "Then he would know that it would be better to have me for a friend than for an enemy. Many men have tried to kill me, many chiefs greater than Nyuto. This is not the first hut in which I have lain a prisoner, nor is it the first time that men have prepared fires to receive me, yet I still live, Lukedi, and many of them are dead. Go, therefore, to Nyuto and advise him to treat me as a friend, for I am not from The Lost Tribe of the Wiramwazi."

"I believe you," said Lukedi, "and I shall go and beg Nyuto to hear me, but I am afraid that he will not."

As the youth reached the doorway of the hut, there suddenly arose a great commotion in the village. Tarzan heard men issuing orders. He heard children crying and the pounding of many naked feet upon the hard ground. Then the war-drums boomed and he heard clashing of weapons upon shields and loud shouting. He saw the guards before the doorway spring to their feet and run to join the other warriors and then Lukedi, at the doorway, shrank back with a cry of terror.

"They come! They come!" he cried, and ran to the far side of the hut where he crouched in terror.

6

ERICH VON HARBEN looked into the faces of the tall, almost naked, warriors whose weapons menaced him across the gunwale of their low dugout, and the first thing to attract his attention was the nature of those weapons.

Their spears were unlike any that he had ever seen in the hands of modern savages. Corresponding with the ordinary spear of the African savage, they carried a heavy and formidable javelin that suggested to the mind of the young archæologist nothing other than the ancient Roman pike, and this similarity was further confirmed by the appearance of the short, broad, two-edged swords that dangled in scabbards supported by straps passing over the left shoulders of the warriors. If this weapon was not the *gladius Hispanus* of the Imperial Legionary, von Harben felt that his studies and researches had been for naught.

"Ask them what they want, Gabula," he directed. "Perhaps they will understand you."

"Who are you and what do you want of us?" demanded Gabula in the Bantu dialect of his tribe.

"We wish to be friends," added von Harben in the same dialect. "We have come to visit your country. Take us to your chief."

A tall Negro in the stern of the dugout shook his head. "I do not understand you," he said. "You are our prisoners. We are going to take you with us to our masters. Come, get into the boat. If you resist or make trouble we shall kill you."

"They speak a strange language," said Gabula. "I do not understand them."

Surprise and incredulity were reflected in the expression on von Harben's face, and he experienced such a sensation as one might who looked upon a man suddenly resurrected after having been dead for nearly two thousand years.

Von Harben had been a close student of ancient Rome and its long dead language, but how different was the living tongue, which he heard and which he recognized for what

36

it was, from the dead and musty pages of ancient manuscripts.

He understood enough of what the man had said to get his meaning, but he recognized the tongue as a hybrid of Latin and Bantu root words, though the inflections appeared to be uniformly those of the Latin language.

In his student days von Harben had often imagined himself a citizen of Rome. He had delivered orations in the Forum and had addressed his troops in the field in Africa and in Gaul, but how different it all seemed now when he was faced with the actuality rather than the figment of imagination. His voice sounded strange in his own ears and his words came haltingly as he spoke to the tall man in the language of the Cæsars.

"We are not enemies," he said. "We have come as friends to visit your country," and then he waited, scarce believing that the man could understand him.

"Are you a citizen of Rome?" demanded the warrior.

"No, but my country is at peace with Rome," replied von Harben.

The man looked puzzled as though he did not understand the reply. "You are from Castra Sanguinarius." His words carried the suggestion of a challenge.

"I am from Germania," replied von Harben.

"I never heard of such a country. You are a citizen of Rome from Castra Sanguinarius."

"Take me to your chief," said von Harben.

"That is what I intend to do. Get in here. Our masters will know what to do with you."

Von Harben and Gabula climbed into the dugout, so awkwardly that they almost overturned it, much to the disgust of the warriors, who seized hold of them none too gently and forced them to squat in the bottom of the frail craft. This was now turned about and paddled along a winding canal, bordered on either side of tufted papyrus rising ten to fifteen feet above the surface of the water.

"To what tribe do you belong?" asked von Harben, addressing the leader of the warriors.

"We are barbarians of the Mare Orientis, subjects of Validus Augustus, Emperor of the East; but why do you ask such questions? You know these things as well as I."

A half hour of steady paddling along winding water-lanes brought them to a collection of beehive huts built upon the floating roots of the papyrus, from which the tall plants had been cleared just sufficiently to make room for the half dozen huts that constituted the village. Here von Harben and Gabula became the center of a curious and excited company of men, women, and children, and von Harben heard himself and Gabula described by their captors as spies from Castra Sanguinarius and learned that on the morrow they were to be taken to Castrum Mare, which he decided must be the village of the mysterious "masters" to whom his captors were continually alluding. The Negroes did not treat them unkindly, though they evidently considered them as enemies.

When they were interviewed by the headman of the village, von Harben, his curiosity aroused, asked him why they had not been molested if all of his people believed, as they seemed to, that they were enemies.

"You are a citizen of Rome," replied the headman, "and this other is your slave. Our masters do not permit us barbarians to injure a citizen of Rome even though he may be from Castra Sanguinarius, except in self-defense or upon the battlefield in time of war."

"Who are your masters?" demanded von Harben.

"Why, the citizens of Rome who live in Castrum Mare, of course, as one from Castra Sanguinarius well knows."

"But I am not from Castra Sanguinarius," insisted von Harben.

"You may tell that to the officers of Validus Augustus," replied the headman. "Perhaps they will believe you, but it is certain that I do not."

"Are these people who dwell in Castrum Mare Negroes?" asked von Harben.

"Take them away," ordered the headman, "and confine them safely in a hut. There they may ask one another foolish questions. I do not care to listen to them further."

Von Harben and Gabula were led away by a group of warriors and conducted into one of the small huts of the village. Here they were brought a supper of fish and snails and a dish concocted of the cooked pith of papyrus.

When morning dawned the prisoners were again served with food similar to that which had been given them the previous evening and shortly thereafter they were ordered from the hut.

Upon the water-lane before the village floated half a dozen dugouts filled with warriors. Their faces and bodies were painted as for war and they appeared to have donned all the finery of barbaric necklaces, anklets, bracelets, armbands, and feathers that each could command; even the prows of the canoes bore odd designs in fresh colors.

There were many more warriors than could have been accommodated in the few huts within the small clearing, but, as von Harben learned later, these came from other clearings, several of which comprised the village. Von Harben and Gabula were ordered into the chief's canoe and a moment later the little fleet pushed off into the water-lane. Strong paddlers propelled the dugouts along the winding waterway in a northeasterly direction.

During the first half hour they passed several small clearings in each of which stood a few huts from which the women and children came to the water's edge to watch them as they passed, but for the most part the water-lane ran between monotonous walls of lofty papyrus, broken only occasionally by short stretches of more open water.

Von Harben tried to draw the chief into conversation, especially relative to their destination and the nature of the "masters" into whose hands they were to be delivered, but the taciturn warrior ignored his every advance and finally von Harben lapsed into the silence of resignation.

They had been paddling for hours, and the heat and monotony had become almost unbearable, when a turn in the water-lane revealed a small body of open water, across the opposite side of which stretched what appeared to be low land surmounted by an earthen rampart, along the top of which was a strong stockade. The course of the canoe was directed toward two lofty towers that apparently marked the gateway through the rampart.

Figures of men could be seen loitering about this gateway, and as they caught sight of the canoes a trumpet sounded and a score of men sallied from the gateway and came down to the water's edge.

As the boat drew nearer, von Harben saw that these men were soldiers, and at the command of one of them the canoes drew up a hundred yards offshore and waited there while the chief shouted to the soldiers on shore telling them who he was and the nature of his business. Permission was then given for the chief's canoe to approach, but the others were ordered to remain where they were.

"Stay where you are," commanded one of the soldiers, evidently an under-officer, as the dugout touched the shore. "I have sent for the centurion."

Von Harben looked with amazement upon the soldiers drawn up at the landing. They wore the tunics and cloaks of Cæsar's legionaries. Upon their feet were the sandal-like caligæ. A helmet, a leather cuirass, an ancient shield with pike and Spanish sword completed the picture of antiquity; only their skin belied the suggestion of their origin. They were not white men; neither were they Negroes, but for the most part of a light-brown color with regular features.

They seemed only mildly curious concerning von Harben, and on the whole appeared rather bored than otherwise. The under-officer questioned the chief concerning conditions in the village. They were casual questions on subjects of no particular moment, but they indicated to von Harben a seemingly interested and friendly relationship between the Negroes of the outlying villages in the papyrus swamp and the evidently civilized brown people of the mainland; yet the fact that only one canoe had been permitted to approach the land suggested that other and less pleasant relations had also existed between them at times. Beyond the rampart von Harben could see the roofs of buildings and far away, beyond these, the towering cliffs that formed the opposite side of the canyon.

Presently two more soldiers emerged from the gateway opposite the landing. One of them was evidently the officer for whom they were waiting, his cloak and cuirass being of finer materials and more elaborately decorated; while the other, who walked a few paces behind him, was a common soldier, probably the messenger who had been dispatched to fetch him.

And now another surprise was added to those which von Harben had already experienced since he had dropped over the edge of the barrier cliffs into this little valley of anachronisms—the officer was unquestionably white.

"Who are these, Rufinus?" he demanded of the underofficer.

"A barbarian chief and warriors from the villages of the western shore," replied Rufinus. "They bring two prisoners that they captured in the Rupes Flumen. As a reward they wish permission to enter the city and see the Emperor."

"How many are they?" asked the officer.

"Sixty," replied Rufinus.

"They may enter the city," said the officer. "I will give them a pass, but they must leave their weapons in their canoes and be out of the city before dark. Send two men with them. As to their seeing Validus Augustus, that I cannot arrange. They might go to the palace and ask the præfect there. Have the prisoners come ashore."

As von Harben and Gabula stepped from the dugout, the expression upon the officer's face was one of perplexity.

"Who are you?" he demanded.

"My name is Erich von Harben," replied the prisoner.

The officer jerked his head impatiently. "There is no such family in Castra Sanguinarius," he retorted.

"I am not from Castra Sanguinarius."

"Not from Castra Sanguinarius!" The officer laughed.

"That is the story he told me," said the chief, who had been listening to the conversation.

"I suppose that he will be saying next that he is not a citizen of Rome," said the officer.

40

"That is just what he does say," said the chief.

"But wait," exclaimed the officer, excitedly. "Perhaps you are indeed from Rome herself!"

"No, I am not from Rome," von Harben assured him.

"Can it be that there are white barbarians in Africa!" exclaimed the officer. "Surely your garments are not Roman. Yes, you must be a barbarian unless, as I suspect, you are not telling me the truth and you are indeed from Castra Sanguinarius."

"A spy, perhaps," suggested Rufinus.

"No," said von Harben. "I am no spy nor am I an emeny," and with a smile, "I am a barbarian, but a friendly barbarian."

"And who is this man?" asked the officer, indicating Gabula. "Your slave?"

"He is my servant, but not a slave."

"Come with me," directed the officer. "I should like to talk with you. I find you interesting, though I do not believe you."

Von Harben smiled. "I do not blame you," he said, "for even though I see you before me I can scarcely believe that you exist."

"I do not understand what you mean," said the officer, "but come with me to my quarters."

He gave orders that Gabula was to be confined in the guardhouse temporarily, and then he led von Harben back to one of the towers that guarded the entrance to the rampart.

The gate lay in a vertical plane at right angles to the rampart with a high tower at either side, the rampart curving inward at this point to connect with the tower at the inner end of the gate. This made a curved entrance that forced an enemy attempting to enter to disclose its right or unprotected side to the defenders upon the rampart, a form of camp fortification that von Harben knew had been peculiar to the ancient Romans.

The officer's quarters consisted of a single, small, bare room directly off a larger room occupied by the members of the guard. It contained a desk, a bench, and a couple of roughly made chairs.

"Sit down," said the officer, after they had entered, "and tell me something about yourself. If you are not from Castra Sanguinarius, from whence do you come? How did you get into our country and what are you doing here?"

"I am from Germania," replied von Harben.

"Bah!" exclaimed the officer. "They are wild and savage barbarians. They do not speak the language of Rome at all; not even as poorly as you."

41

"How recently have you come in contact with German barbarians?" von Harben asked.

"Oh, I? Never, of course, but our historians knew them well."

"And how lately have they written of them?"

"Why, Sanguinarius himself mentions them in the story of his life."

"Sanguinarius?" questioned von Harben. "I do not recall ever having heard of him."

"Sanguinarius fought against the barbarians of Germania in the 839th year of Rome."

"That was about eighteen hundred and thirty-seven years ago," von Harben reminded the officer, "and I think you will have to admit that there may have been much progress in that time."

"And why?" demanded the other. "There have been no changes in this country since the days of Sanguinarius and he has been dead over eighteen hundred years. It is not likely then that barbarians would change greatly if Roman citizens have not. You say you are from Germania. Perhaps you were taken to Rome as a captive and got your civilization there, but your apparel is strange. It is not of Rome. It is not of any place of which I have ever heard. Go on with your story."

"My father is a medical missionary in Africa," explained von Harben. "Often when I have visited him I heard the story of a lost tribe that was supposed to live in these mountains. The natives told strange stories of a white race living in the depths of the Wiramwazi. They said that the mountains were inhabited by the ghosts of their dead. Briefly, I came to investigate the story. All but one of my men, terrified after we reached the outer slopes of the mountains, deserted me. That one and I managed to descend to the floor of the canyon. Immediately we were captured and brought here."

For a while the other sat in silence, thinking.

"Perhaps you are telling me the truth," he said, at last. "Your apparel is not that of Castra Sanguinarius and you speak our language with such a peculiar accent and with so great effort that it is evidently not your mother tongue. I shall have to report your capture to the Emperor, but in the meantime I shall take you to the home of my uncle, Septimus Favonius. If he believes your story he can help you, as he has great influence with the Emperor, Validus Augustus."

"You are kind," said von Harben, "and I shall need a friend here if the customs of Imperial Rome still prevail in your country, as you suggest. Now that you know so much

42

about me, perhaps you will tell me something about yourself."

"There is little to tell," said the officer. "My name is Mallius Lepus. I am a centurion in the army of Validus Augustus. Perhaps, if you are familiar with Roman customs, you will wonder that a patrician should be a centurion, but in this matter as in some others we have not followed the customs of Rome. Sanguinarius admitted all his centurions to the patrician class, and since then for over eighteen hundred years only patricians have been appointed centurions.

"But here is Aspar," exclaimed Mallius Lepus, as another officer entered the room. "He has come to relieve me and when he has taken over the gate you and I shall go at once to the home of my uncle, Septimus Favonius."

7

TARZAN OF THE APES looked at Lukedi in surprise and then out through the low doorway of the hut in an effort to see what it was that had so filled the breast of the youth with terror.

The little section of the village street, framed by the doorway, showed a milling mass of brown bodies, waving spears, terrified women and children. What could it mean?

At first he thought that Lukedi meant that the Bagegos were coming for Tarzan, but now he guessed that the Bagegos were being beset by troubles of their own, and at last he came to the conclusion that some other savage tribe had attacked the village.

But, whatever the cause of the uproar, it was soon over. He saw the Bagegos turn and flee in all directions. Strange figures passed before his eyes in pursuit, and for a time there was comparative silence, only a hurrying of feet, an occasional command and now and then a scream of terror.

Presently three figures burst into the hut—enemy warriors searching the village for fugitives. Lukedi, trembling, inarticulate, paralyzed by fright, crouched against the far wall. Tarzan sat leaning against the center pole to which he was chained. At sight of him, the leading warrior halted, surprise written upon his face. His fellows joined him and they stood for a moment in excited conversation, evidently discussing their find. Then one of them addressed Tarzan, but in a tongue that the ape-man could not understand, although he realized that there was something vaguely and tantalizingly familiar about it.

Then one of them discovered Lukedi and, crossing the hut, dragged him to the center of the floor. They spoke again to Tarzan, motioning him toward the door so that he understood that they were ordering him from the hut, but in reply he pointed to the chain about his neck.

One of the warriors examined the lock that secured the chain, spoke to his fellows, and then left the hut. He returned very shortly with two rocks and, making Tarzan lie upon the ground, placed the padlock upon one of the rocks and pounded upon it with the other until it broke.

As soon as he was released, Tarzan and Lukedi were ordered from the hut, and when they had come out into the open the ape-man had an opportunity to examine his captors more closely. In the center of the village there were about one hundred light-brown warriors surrounding their Bagego prisoners, of whom there were some fifty men, women, and children.

The tunics, cuirasses, helmets, and sandals of the raiders Tarzan knew that he had never seen before, and yet they were as vaguely familiar as was the language spoken by their wearers.

The heavy spears and the swords hanging at their right sides were not precisely like any spears or swords that he had ever seen, and yet he had a feeling that they were not entirely unfamiliar objects. The effect of the appearance of these strangers was tantalizing in the extreme. It is not uncommon for us to have experiences that are immediately followed by such a sensation of familiarity that we could swear we had lived through them before in their minutest detail, and yet we are unable to recall the time or place or any coincident occurrences.

It was such a sensation that Tarzan experienced now. He thought that he had seen these men before, that he had heard them talk; he almost felt that at some time he had understood their language, and yet at the same time he knew that he had never seen them. Then a figure approached from the opposite side of the village—a white man, garbed similarly to the warriors, but in more resplendent trappings, and of a sudden Tarzan of the Apes found the key and the solution of the mystery, for the man who came toward him might have stepped from the pedestal of the statue of Julius Cæsar in the Palazzo dei Conservatori in Rome.

These were Romans! A thousand years after the fall of Rome he had been captured by a band of Cæsar's legionaries, and now he knew why the language was so vaguely familiar, for Tarzan, in his effort to fit himself for a place in the civilized world into which necessity sometimes commanded him, had studied many things and among them Latin, but the reading of Cæsar's Commentaries and scanning Vergil do not give one a command of the language and so Tarzan could neither speak nor understand the spoken words, though the smattering that he had of the language was sufficient to make it sound familiar when he heard others speaking it.

Tarzan looked intently at the Cæsar-like white man approaching him and at the dusky, stalwart legionaries about him. He shook himself. This indeed must be a dream, and then he saw Lukedi with the other Bagego prisoners. He saw the stake that had been set up for his burning and he knew that as these were realities so were the strange warriors about him.

Each soldier carried a short length of chain, at one end of which was a metal collar and a padlock, and with these they were rapidly chaining the prisoners neck to neck.

While they were thus occupied the white man, who was evidently an officer, was joined by two other whites similarly garbed. The three caught sight of Tarzan and immediately approached and questioned him, but the ape-man shook his head to indicate that he could not understand their language. Then they questioned the soldiers who had discovered him in the hut and finally the commander of the company issued some instructions relative to the ape-man and turned away.

The result was that Tarzan was not chained to the file of prisoners, but though he again wore the iron collar, the end of the chain was held by one of the legionaries in whose keeping he had evidently been placed.

Tarzan could only believe that this preferential treatment was accorded him because of his color and the reluctance of the white officers to chain another white with Negroes.

As the raiders marched away from the village one of the officers and a dozen legionaries marched in advance. These were followed by the long line of prisoners accompanied by another officer and a small guard. Behind the prisoners, many of whom were compelled to carry the live chickens that were a part of the spoils of the raid, came another contingent of soldiers herding the cows and goats and sheep of the villagers, and behind all a large rear guard comprising the greater part of the legionaries under the command of the third officer.

The march led along the base of the mountains in a northerly direction and presently upward diagonally across

45

the rising slopes at the west end of the Wiramwazi range.

It chanced that Tarzan's position was at the rear of the line of prisoners, at the end of which marched Lukedi.

"Who are these people, Lukedi?" asked Tarzan, after the party had settled down to steady progress.

"These are the ghost people of the Wiramwazi," replied the young Bagego.

"They have come to prevent the killing of their fellow," said another, looking at Tarzan. "I knew Nyuto should not have made him prisoner. I knew that harm would come from it. It is well for us that the ghost people came before we had slain him."

"What difference will it make?" said another. "I would rather have been killed in my own village than to be taken into the country of the ghost people and killed there."

"Perhaps they will not kill us," suggested Tarzan.

"They will not kill you because you are one of them, but they will kill the Bagegos because they did dare to take you prisoner."

"But they have taken him prisoner, too," said Lukedi. "Can you not see that he is not one of them? He does not even understand their language."

The other men shook their heads, but they were not convinced. They had made up their minds that Tarzan was one of the ghost people and they were determined that nothing should alter this conviction.

After two hours of marching the trail turned sharply to the right and entered a narrow and rocky gorge, the entrance to which was so choked with trees and undergrowth that it could not have been visible from any point upon the slopes below.

The gorge soon narrowed until its rocky walls could be spanned by a man's outstretched arms. The floor, strewn with jagged bits of granite from the lofty cliffs above, afforded poor and dangerous footing, so that the speed of the column was greatly reduced.

As they proceeded Tarzan realized that, although they were entering more deeply into the mountains, the trend of the gorge was downward rather than upward. The cliffs on either side rose higher and higher above them until in places the gloom of night surrounded them and, far above, the stars twinkled in the morning sky.

For a long hour they followed the windings of the dismal gorge. The column halted for a minute or two and immediately after the march was resumed Tarzan saw those directly ahead of him filing through an arched gateway in the man-made wall of solid masonry that entirely blocked the gorge to a height of at least a hundred feet. Also, when it was the ape-man's turn to pass the portal, he saw that it was guarded by other soldiers similar to those into whose hands he had fallen and that it was further re-enforced by a great gate of huge, hand-hewn timbers that had been swung open to permit the party pass.

Ahead of him Tarzan saw a well-worn road leading down into a dense forest in which huge, live oaks predominated, though interspersed with other varieties of trees, among which he recognized acacias and a variety of plane tree as well as a few cedars.

Shortly after passing through the gate the officer in charge gave the command to halt at a small village of conical huts that was inhabited by Negroes not unlike the Bagegos, but armed with pikes and swords similar to those carried by the legionaries.

Preparations were immediately made to camp in the village, the natives turning over their huts to the soldiers, quite evidently, judging from the expressions on their faces, with poor grace. The legionaries took possession of whatever they wished and ordered their hosts about with all the authority and assurance of conquerors.

At this village a ration of corn and dried fish was issued to the prisoners. They were given no shelter, but were permitted to gather deadwood and build a fire, around which they clustered, still chained neck to neck.

Numerous birds, strange to Tarzan, flitted among the branches of the trees overhead and numerous monkeys chattered and scolded, but monkeys were no novelty to Tarzan of the Apes, who was far more interested in noting the manners and customs of his captors.

Presently an acorn fell upon Tarzan's head, but as acorns might be expected to fall from oak trees he paid no attention to the occurrence until a second and third acorn in rapid succession struck him squarely from above, and then he glanced up to see a little monkey perched upon a low branch just above him.

"So-o, Nkima!" he exclaimed. "How did you get here?"

"I saw them take you from the village of the Gomangani. I followed."

"You came through the gorge, Nkima?"

"Nkima was afraid that the rocks would come together and crush him," said the little monkey, "so he climbed to the top and came over the mountains along the edge. Far, far below he could hear the Tarmangani and the Gomangani walking along the bottom. Away up there the wind blew and little Nkima was cold and the spoor of Sheeta the leopard was everywhere and there were great baboons who chased little Nkima, so that he was glad when he came to the end of the mountain and saw the forest far below. It was a very steep mountain. Even little Nkima was afraid, but he found the way to the bottom."

"Nkima had better run home," said Tarzan. "This forest is full of strange monkeys."

"I am not afraid," said Nkima. "They are little monkeys and they are all afraid of Nkima. They are homely little monkeys. They are not so beautiful as Nkima, but Nkima has seen some of the shes looking at him and admiring him. It is not a bad place for Nkima. What are the strange Tarmangani going to do with Tarzan of the Apes?"

"I do not know, Nkima," said the ape-man.

"Then Nkima will go back and fetch Muviro and the Waziri."

"No," said the ape-man. "Wait until I find the Tarmangani for whom we are searching. Then you may go back with a message for Muviro."

That night Tarzan and the other prisoners slept upon the hard ground in the open and, after it was dark, little Nkima came down and snuggled in his master's arms and there he lay all night, happy to be near the great Tarmangani he loved.

As morning dawned, Ogonyo, who had been captured with the other Bagegos, opened his eyes and looked about him. The camp of the soldiers was just stirring. Ogonyo saw some of the legionaries emerging from the huts that they had commandeered. He saw his fellow prisoners huddled close together for warmth and at a little distance from them lay the white man whom he had so recently guarded in the prison hut in the village of Nyuto, his chief. As his eyes rested upon the white man, he saw the head of a little monkey arise from the encircling arms of the sleeper. He saw it cast a glance in the direction of the legionaries emerging from the huts and then he saw it scamper quickly to a near-by tree and swing quickly into the branches above.

Ogonyo gave a cry of alarm that awakened the prisoners near him.

"What is the matter, Ogonyo?" cried one of them.

"The ghost of my grandfather!" he exclaimed. "I saw him again. He came out of the mouth of the white man who calls himself Tarzan. He has put a curse upon us because we kept the white man prisoner. Now we are prisoners ourselves and soon we shall be killed and eaten." The others nodded their heads solemnly in confirmation.

Food similar to that given to them the night before was given to the prisoners, and after they and the legionaries had eaten, the march was resumed in a southerly direction along the dusty road.

Until noon they plodded through the dust toward the south,

passing through other villages similar to that at which they had camped during the night, and then they turned directly east into a road that joined the main road at this point. Shortly afterward Tarzan saw before him, stretching across the road to the right and left as far as he could see through the forest, a lofty rampart surmounted by palisades and battlements. Directly ahead the roadway swung to the left just inside the outer line of the rampart and passed through a gateway that was flanked by lofty towers. At the base of the rampart was a wide moat through which a stream of water moved slowly, the moat being spanned by a bridge where the road crossed it.

There was a brief halt at the gateway while the officer commanding the company conferred with the commander of the gate, and then the legionaries and their prisoners filed through and Tarzan saw stretching before him not a village of native huts, but a city of substantial buildings.

Those near the gate were one-story stucco houses, apparently built around an inner courtyard, as he could see the foliage of trees rising high above the roofs, but at a distance down the vista of a long avenue he saw the outlines of more imposing edifices rising to a greater height.

As they proceeded along the avenue they saw many people upon the streets and in the doorways of the houses—brown and black people, clothed for the most part in tunics and cloaks, though many of the Negroes were almost naked. In the vicinity of the gateway there were a few shops, but as they proceeded along the avenue these gave way to dwellings that continued for a considerable distance until they reached a section that seemed to be devoted to shops of a better grade and to public buildings. Here they began to encounter white men, though the proportion of them to the total population seemed quite small.

The people they passed stopped to look at the legionaries and their prisoners and at intersections little crowds formed and quite a number followed them, but these were mostly small boys.

The ape-man could see that he was attracting a great deal of attention and the people seemed to be commenting and speculating upon him. Some of them called to the legionaries, who answered them good-naturedly, and there was considerable joking and chaffing—probably, Tarzan surmised, at the expense of the unfortunate prisoners.

During the brief passage through the city Tarzan came to the conclusion that the Negro inhabitants were the servants, perhaps slaves; the brown men, the soldiers and shopkeepers, while the whites formed the aristocratic or patrician class.

Well within the city the company turned to the left

49

into another broad avenue and shortly afterward approached a great circular edifice constructed of hewn granite blocks. Arched apertures flanked by graceful columns rose tier upon tier to a height of forty or fifty feet, and above the first story all of these arches were open. Through them Tarzan could see that the enclosure was without a roof and he guessed that this lofty wall enclosed an arena, since it bore a marked resemblance to the Colosseum at Rome.

As they came opposite the building the head of the column turned and entered it beneath a low, wide arch and here they were led through numerous corridors in the first story of the building and down a flight of granite steps into gloomy, subterranean chambers, where, opening from a long corridor, the ends of which were lost in darkness in both directions, were a series of narrow doorways before which swung heavy iron gates. In parties of four or five the prisoners were unchained and ordered into the dungeons that lay behind.

Tarzan found himself with Lukedi and two other Bagegos in a small room constructed entirely of granite blocks. The only openings were the narrow, grated doorway, through which they entered, and a small, grated window in the top of the wall opposite the door, and through this window came a little light and air. The grating was closed upon them, the heavy padlock snapped, and they were left alone to wonder what fate lay in store for them.

8

MALLIUS LEPUS conducted von Harben from the quarters of the captain of the gate in the south wall of the island city of Castrum Mare and, summoning a soldier, bade him fetch Gabula.

"You shall come with me as my guest, Erich von Harben," announced Mallius Lepus, "and, by Jupiter, unless I am mistaken, Septimus Favonius will thank me for bringing such a find. His dinners lag for want of novelty, for long since has he exhausted all the possibilities of Castrum Mare. He has even had a Negro chief from the Western forest as his guest of honor, and once he invited the aristocracy of Castrum Mare to meet a great ape.

"His friends will be mad to meet a barbarian chief

from Germania—you are a chief, are you not?" and as von Harben was about to reply, Mallius Lepus stayed him with a gesture. "Never mind! You shall be introduced as a chief and if I do not know any different I cannot be accused of falsifying."

Von Harben smiled as he realized how alike was human nature the world over and in all periods of time.

"Here is your slave now," said Mallius. "As the guest of Septimus Favonius you will have others to do your bidding, but doubtless you will want to have your own body-servant as well."

"Yes," said von Harben. "Gabula has been very faithful. I should hate to part with him."

Mallius led the way to a long shed-like building beneath the inner face of the rampart. Here were two litters and a number of strapping bearers. As Mallius appeared eight of these sprang to their stations in front and behind one one of the litters and carried it from the shed, lowering it to the ground again before their master.

"And tell me, if you have visited Rome recently, does my litter compare favorably with those now used by the nobles?" demanded Mallius.

"There have been many changes, Mallius Lepus, since the Rome of which your historian, Sanguinarius, wrote. Were I to tell you of even the least of them, I fear that you would not believe me."

"But certainly there could have been no great change in the style of litters," argued Mallius, "and I cannot believe that the patricians have ceased to use them."

"Their litters travel upon wheels now," said von Harben.

"Incredible!" exclaimed Mallius. "It would be torture to bump over the rough pavements and country roads on the great wooden wheels of ox-carts. No, Erich von Harben, I am afraid I cannot believe that story."

"The city pavements are smooth today and the country side is cut in all directions by wide, level highways over which the litters of the modern citizens of Rome roll at great speed on small wheels with soft tires—nothing like the great wooden wheels of the ox-carts you have in mind, Mallius Lepus."

The officer called a command to his carriers, who broke into a smart run.

"I warrant you, Erich von Harben, that there be no litters in all Rome that move at greater speed than this," he boasted.

"How fast are we traveling now?" asked von Harben.

"Better than eighty-five hundred paces an hour," replied Mallius.

"Fifty thousand paces an hour is nothing unusual for the

wheeled litters of today," said von Harben. "We call them automobiles."

"You are going to be a great success," cried Mallius, slapping von Harben upon the shoulder. "May Jupiter strike me dead if the guests of Septimus Favonius do not say that I have made a find indeed. Tell them that there be litter-carriers in Rome today who can run fifty thousand paces in an hour and they will acclaim you the greatest entertainer as well as the greatest liar Castrum Mare has ever seen."

Von Harben laughed good-naturedly. "But you will have to admit, my friend, that I never said that there were litter-bearers who could run fifty thousand paces an hour," he reminded Mallius.

"But did you not assure me that the litters traveled that fast? How then may a litter travel unless it is carried by bearers. Perhaps the litters of today are carried by horses. Where are the horses that can run fifty thousand paces in an hour?"

"The litters are neither carried nor drawn by horses or men, Mallius," said von Harben.

The officer leaned back against the soft cushion of the carriage, roaring with laughter. "They fly then, I presume," he jeered. "By Hercules, you must tell this all over again to Septimus Favonius. I promise you that he will love you."

They were passing along a broad avenue bordered by old trees. There was no pavement and the surface of the street was deep with dust. The houses were built quite up to the street line and where there was space between adjacent houses a high wall closed the aperture, so that each side of the street presented a solid front of masonry broken by arched gateways, heavy doors, and small unglazed windows, heavily barred.

"These are residences?" asked von Harben, indicating the buildings they were passing.

"Yes," said Mallius.

"From the massive doors and heavily barred windows I should judge that your city is overrun with criminals," commented von Harben.

Mallius shook his head. "On the contrary," he said, "we have few criminals in Castrum Mare. The defenses that you see are against the possible uprising of slaves or invasions by barbarians. Upon several occasions during the life of the city such things have occurred, and so we build to safeguard against disaster in the event that there should be a recurrence of them, but, even so, doors are seldom locked, even at night, for there are no thieves to break in, no criminals to menace the lives of our people. If a man has done wrong to a fellow man he may have reason to expect the dagger of the assassin, but if his conscience be cleared he may live without fear of attack."

"I cannot conceive of a city without criminals," said von Harben. "How do you account for it?"

"That is simple," replied Mallius. "When Honus Hasta revolted and founded the city of Castrum Mare in the 953rd year of Rome, Castra Sanguinarius was overrun with criminals, so that no man dared go abroad at night without an armed body-guard, nor was any one safe within his own home, and Honus Hasta, who became the first Emperor of the East, swore that there should be no criminals in Castrum Mare and he made laws so drastic that no thief or murderer lived to propagate his kind. Indeed, the laws of Honus Hasta destroyed not only the criminal, but all the members of his family, so that there was none to transmit to posterity the criminal inclinations of a depraved sire.

"There are many who thought Honus Hasta a cruel tyrant, but time has shown the widsom of many of his acts and certainly our freedom from criminals may only be ascribed to the fact that the laws of Honus Hasta prevented the breeding of criminals. So seldom now does an individual arise who steals or wantonly murders that it is an event of as great moment as any that can occur, and the entire city takes a holiday to see the culprit and his family destroyed."

Entering an avenue of more pretentious homes, the litter-bearers halted before an ornate gate where Lepus and Erich descended from the litter. In answer to the summons of the former, the gate was opened by a slave and von Harben followed his new friend across a tiled forecourt into an inner garden, where beneath the shade of a tree a stout, elderly man was writing at a low desk. It was with something of a thrill that von Harben noted the ancient Roman inkstand, the reed pen, and the roll of parchment that the man was using as naturally as though they had not been quite extinct for a thousand years.

"Greetings, Uncle!" cried Lepus, and as the older man turned toward them, "I have brought you a guest such as no citizen of Castrum Mare has entertained since the founding of the city. This, my uncle, is Erich von Harben, barbarian chief from far Germania." Then to von Harben, "My revered uncle, Septimus Favonius."

Septimus Favonius arose and greeted von Harben hospitably, yet with such a measure of conscious dignity as to carry the suggestion that a barbarian, even though a chief and a guest, could not be received upon a plane of actual social equality by a citizen of Rome.

Very briefly Lepus recounted the occurrences leading to

his meeting with von Harben. Septimus Favonius seconded his nephew's invitation to be their guest, and then, at the suggestion of the older man, Lepus took Erich to his apartments to outfit him with fresh apparel.

An hour later, Erich, shaved and appareled as a young Roman patrician, stepped from the apartment, which had been placed at his disposal, into the adjoining chamber, which was a part of the suite of Mallius Lepus.

"Go on down to the garden," said Lepus, "and when I am dressed I shall join you there."

As von Harben passed through the home of Septimus Favonius on his way to the garden court, he was impressed by the peculiar blending of various cultures in the architecture and decoration of the home.

The walls and columns of the building followed the simplest Grecian lines of architecture, while the rugs, hangings, and mural decorations showed marked evidence of both oriental and savage African influences. The latter he could understand, but the source of the oriental designs in many of the decorations was quite beyond him, since it was obvious that The Lost Tribe had had no intercourse with the outside world, other than with the savage Bagegos, for many centuries.

And when he stepped out into the garden, which was of considerable extent, he saw a further blending of Rome and savage Africa, for while the main part of the building was roofed with handmade tile, several porches were covered with native grass thatch, while a small outbuilding at the far end of the garden was a replica of a Bagego hut except that the walls were left unplastered, so that the structure appeared in the nature of a summer-house. Septimus Favonius had left the garden and von Harben took advantage of the fact to examine his surroundings more closely. The garden was laid out with winding, graveled walks, bordered by shrubs and flowers, with an occasional tree, some of which gave evidence of great age.

The young man's mind, his eyes, his imagination were so fully occupied with his surroundings that he experienced a sensation almost akin to shock as he followed the turning of the path around a large ornamental shrub and came face to face with a young woman.

That she was equally surprised was evidenced by the consternation apparent in her expression as she looked wide-eyed into the eyes of von Harben. For quite an appreciable moment of time they stood looking at one another. Von Harben thought that never in his life had he seen so beautiful a girl. What the girl thought, von Harben did not know. It was she who broke the silence.

"Who are you?" she asked, in a voice little above a whisper, as one might conceivably address an apparition that had arisen suddenly and unexpectedly before him.

"I am a stranger here," replied von Harben, "and I owe you an apology for intruding upon your privacy. I thought that I was alone in the garden."

"Who are you?" repeated the girl. "I have never seen your face before or one like yours."

"And I," said von Harben, "have never seen a girl like you. Perhaps I am dreaming. Perhaps you do not exist at all, for it does not seem credible that in the world of realities such a one as you could exist."

The girl blushed. "You are not of Castrum Mare," she said. "That I can see." Her tone was a trifle cold and slightly haughty.

"I have offended you," said von Harben. "I ask your pardon. I did not mean to be offensive, but coming upon you so unexpectedly quite took my breath away."

"And your manners, too?" asked the girl, but now her eyes were smiling.

"You have forgiven me?" asked von Harben.

"You will have to tell me who you are and why you are here before I can answer that," she replied. "For all I know you might be an enemy or a barbarian."

Von Harben laughed. "Mallius Lepus, who invited me here, insists that I am a barbarian," he said, "but even so I am the guest of Septimus Favonius, his uncle."

The girl shrugged. "I am not surprised," she said. "My father is notorious for the guests he honors."

"You are the daughter of Favonius?" asked von Harben.

"Yes, I am Favonia," replied the girl, "but you have not yet told me about yourself. I command you to do so," she said, imperiously.

"I am Erich von Harben of Germania," said the young man.

"Germania!" exclaimed the girl. "Cæsar wrote of Germania, as did Sanguinarius. It seems very far away."

"It never seemed so far as now," said von Harben; "yet the three thousand miles of distance seem nothing by comparison with the centuries of time that intervene."

The girl puckered her brows. "I do not understand you," she said.

"No," said von Harben, "and I cannot blame you."

"You are a chief, of course?" she asked.

He did not deny the insinuation, for he had been quick to see from the attitude of the three patricians he had met that the social standing of a barbarian in Castrum Mare might be easily open to question, unless his barbarism was some-

55

what mitigated by a title. Proud as he was of his nationality, von Harben realized that it was a far cry from the European barbarians of Cæsar's day to their cultured descendants of the twentieth century and that it would probably be impossible to convince these people of the changes that have taken place since their history was written; and, also, he was conscious of a very definite desire to appear well in the eyes of this lovely maiden of a bygone age.

"Favonia!" exclaimed von Harben. He scarcely breathed the name.

The girl looked up at him questioningly. "Yes!" she said.

"It is such a lovely name," he said. "I never heard it spoken before."

"You like it?" she asked.

"Very much, indeed."

The girl puckered her brows in thought. She had beautiful penciled brows and a forehead that denoted an intelligence that was belied by neither her eyes, her manner, nor her speech. "I am glad that you like my name, but I do not understand why I should be glad. You say that you are a barbarian, and yet you do not seem like a barbarian. Your appearance and your manner are those of a patrician, though perhaps you are overbold with a young woman you have never met before, but that I ascribe to the ignorance of the barbarian and so I forgive it."

"Being a barbarian has its compensations," laughed von Harben, "and perhaps I am a barbarian. I may be again forgiven if I say you are quite the most beautiful girl I have ever seen and the only one—I could—," he hesitated.

"You could what?" she demanded.

"Even a barbarian should not dare to say what I was about to say to one whom I have known scarce half a dozen minutes."

"Whoever you may be, you show rare discrimination," came in a sarcastic tone in a man's voice directly behind von Harben.

The girl looked up in surprise and von Harben wheeled about simultaneously, for neither had been aware of the presence of another. Facing him von Harben saw a short, dark, greasy-looking young man in an elaborate tunic, his hand resting upon the hilt of the short sword that hung at his hip. There was a sarcastic sneer upon the face of the newcomer.

"Who is your barbarian friend, Favonia?" he demanded.

"This is Erich von Harben, a guest in the home of Septimus Favonius, my father," replied the girl, haughtily; and to von Harben, "This is Fulvus Fupus, who accepts the hospitality of Septimus Favonius so often that he feels free to criticize another guest."

Fupus flushed. "I apologize," he said, "but one may never know when to honor or when to ridicule one of Septimus Favonius's guests of honor. The last, if I recall correctly, was an ape, and before that there was a barbarian from some outer village—but they are always interesting and I am sure that the barbarian, Erich von Harben, will prove no exception to the rule." The man's tone was sarcastic and obnoxious to a degree, and it was with difficulty that von Harben restrained his mounting temper.

Fortunately, at this moment, Mallius Lepus joined them and von Harben was formally presented to Favonia. Fulvus Fupus thereafter paid little attention to von Harben, but devoted his time assiduously to Favonia. Von Harben knew from their conversation that they were upon friendly and intimate terms and he guessed that Fupus was in love with Favonia, though he could not tell from the girl's attitude whether or not she returned his affection.

There was something else that von Harben was sure of —that he too was in love with Favonia. Upon several occasions in life he had thought that he was in love, but his sensations and reactions upon those other occasions had not been the same in either kind or degree as those which he now experienced. He found himself hating Fulvus Fupus, whom he had known scarce a quarter of an hour and whose greatest offense, aside from looking lovingly at Favonia, had been a certain arrogant sarcasm of speech and manner— certainly no sufficient warrant for a sane man to wish to do murder, and yet Erich von Harben fingered the butt of his Luger, which he had insisted upon wearing in addition to the slim dagger with which Mallius Lepus had armed him.

Later, when Septimus Favonius joined them, he suggested that they all go to the baths and Mallius Lepus whispered to von Harben that his uncle was already itching to exhibit his new find.

"He will take us to the Baths of Cæsar," said Lepus, "which are patronized by the richest patricians only, so have a few good stories ready, but save your best ones, like that you told me about the modern Roman litters, for the dinner that my uncle is sure to give tonight—for he will have the best of Castrum Mare there, possibly even the Emperor himself."

The Baths of Cæsar were housed in an imposing building, of which that portion facing on the avenue was given over to what appeared to be exclusive shops. The main entrance led to a large court where the warmth with which the party was greeted by a number of patrons of the Baths already congregated there attested to the popularity of Favonius, his daughter, and his nephew, while it was evident to von Harben that there was less enthusiasm manifested for Fulvus Fupus.

Servants conducted the bathers to the dressing-rooms, the men's and women's being in different quarters of the building.

After his clothes were removed, von Harben's body was anointed with oils in a warm room and then he was led into a hot room and from there with the other men he passed into a large apartment containing a plunge where both the men and women gathered. About the plunge were seats for several hundred people, and in the Baths of Cæsar these were constructed of highly polished granite.

While von Harben enjoyed the prospect of a swim in the clear, cold water of the frigidarium, he was much more interested by the opportunity it afforded him to be with Favonia again. She was swimming slowly around the pool when he entered the room and, making a long, running dive, von Harben slipped easily and gracefully into the water, a few strokes bringing him to her side. A murmur of applause that followed meant nothing to von Harben, for he did not know that diving was an unknown art among the citizens of Castrum Mare.

Fulvus Fupus, who had entered the frigidarium behind von Harben, sneered as he saw the dive and heard the applause. He had never seen it done before, but he could see that the thing was very easy, and realizing the advantages of so graceful an accomplishment, he determined at once to show the assembled patricians, and especially Favonia, that he was equally a master of this athletic art as was the barbarian.

Running, as he had seen von Harben run, toward the edge of the pool, Fulvus Fupus sprang high into the air and came straight down upon his belly with a resounding smack that sent the wind out of him and the water splashing high in all directions.

Gasping for breath, he managed to reach the side of the pool, where he clung while the laughter of the assembled patricians brought the scarlet of mortification to his face. Whereas before he had viewed von Harben with contempt and some slight suspicion, he now viewed him with contempt, suspicion, and hatred. Disgruntled, Fupus clambered from the pool and returned immediately to the dressing-room, where he donned his garments.

"Going already, Fupus?" demanded a young patrician who was disrobing in the apodyterium.

"Yes," growled Fupus.

"I hear you came with Septimus Favonius and his new find. What sort may he be?"

"Listen well, Cæcilius Metellus," said Fupus. "This man who calls himself Erich von Harben says that he is a chief from Germania, but I believe otherwise."

"What do you believe?" demanded Metellus, politely, though evidently with no considerable interest.

Fupus came close to the other. "I believe him to be a spy from Castra Sanguinarius," he whispered, "and that he is only pretending that he is a barbarian."

"But they say that he does not speak our language well," said Metellus.

"He speaks it as any man might speak it who wanted to pretend that he did not understand it or that it was new to him," said Fupus.

Metellus shook his head. "Septimus Favonius is no fool," he said. "I doubt if there is anyone in Castra Sanguinarius sufficiently clever to fool him to such an extent."

"There is only one man who has any right to judge as to that," snapped Fupus, "and he is going to have the facts before I am an hour older."

"Whom do you mean?" asked Metellus.

"Validus Augustus, Emperor of the East—I am going to him at once."

"Don't be a fool, Fupus," counseled Metellus. "You will only get yourself laughed at or possibly worse. Know you not that Septimus Favonius is high in the favor of the Emperor?"

"Perhaps, but is it not also known that he was friendly with Cassius Hasta, nephew of the Emperor, whom Validus Augustus accused of treason and banished. It would not take much to convince the Emperor that this Erich von Harben is an emissary of Cassius Hasta, who is reputed to be in Castra Sanguinarius."

Cæcilius Metellus laughed. "Go on then and make a fool of yourself, Fupus," he said. "You will probably bring up at the end of a rope."

"The end of a rope will terminate this business," agreed Fupus, "but von Harben will be there, not I."

9

As night fell upon the city of Castra Sanguinarius, the gloom of the granite dungeons beneath the city's Colosseum deepened into blackest darkness, which was relieved only by a rectangular patch of starlit sky where barred windows pierced the walls.

Squatting upon the rough stone floor, his back against the wall, Tarzan watched the stars moving in slow procession across the window's opening. A creature of the wild, impatient of restraint, the ape-man suffered the mental anguish of the caged beast—perhaps, because of his human mind, his suffering was greater than would have been that of one of the lower orders, yet he endured with even greater outward stoicism than the beast that paces to and fro seeking escape from the bars that confine it.

As the feet of the beast might have measured the walls of its dungeon, so did the mind of Tarzan, and never for a waking moment was his mind not occupied by thoughts of escape.

Lukedi and the other inmates of the dungeon slept, but Tarzan still sat watching the free stars and envying them, when he became conscious of a sound, ever so slight, coming from the arena, the floor of which was about on a level with the sill of the little window in the top of the dungeon wall. Something was moving, stealthily and cautiously, upon the sand of the arena. Presently, framed in the window, silhouetted against the sky, appeared a familiar figure. Tarzan smiled and whispered a word so low that a human ear could scarce have heard it, and Nkima slipped between the bars and dropped to the floor of the dungeon. An instant later the little monkey snuggled close to Tarzan, its long, muscular arms clasped tightly about the neck of the ape-man.

"Come home with me," pleaded Nkima. "Why do you stay in this cold, dark hole beneath the ground?"

"You have seen the cage in which we sometimes keep Jad-Bal-Ja, the Golden Lion?" demanded Tarzan.

"Yes," said Nkima.

"Jad-Bal-Ja cannot get out unless we open the gate," explained Tarzan. "I too am in a cage. I cannot get out until they open the gate."

"I will go and get Muviro and his Gomangani with the sharp sticks," said Nkima. "They will come and let you out."

"No, Nkima," said Tarzan. "If I cannot get out by myself, Muviro could not get here in time to free me, and if he came many of my brave Waziri would be killed, for there are fighting men here in far greater numbers than Muviro could bring." After awhile Tarzan slept, and curled up within his arms slept Nkima, the little monkey, but when Tarzan awoke in the morning Nkima was gone.

Toward the middle of the morning soldiers came and the door of the dungeon was unlocked and opened to admit several of them, including a young white officer, who was accompanied by a slave. The officer addressed Tarzan in the language of the city, but the ape-man shook his head, indicating that he did not understand; then the other turned to the slave with a few words and the latter spoke to Tarzan in the Bagego dialect, asking him if he understood it.

"Yes," replied the ape-man, and through the interpreter the officer questioned Tarzan.

"Who are you and what were you, a white man, doing in the village of the Bagegos?" asked the officer.

"I am Tarzan of the Apes," replied the prisoner. "I was looking for another white man who is lost somewhere in these mountains, but I slipped upon the cliffside and fell and while I was unconscious the Bagegos took me prisoner, and when your soldiers raided the Bagego village they found me there. Now that you know about me, I presume that I shall be released."

"Why?" demanded the officer. "Are you a citizen of Rome?"

"Of course not," said Tarzan. "What has that to do with it?"

"Because if you are not a citizen of Rome it is quite possible that you are an enemy. How do we know that you are not from Castrum Mare?"

Tarzan shrugged. "I do not know," he said, "how you would know that since I do not even know what Castrum Mare means."

"That is what you would say if you wished to deceive us," said the officer, "and you would also pretend that you could not speak or understand our language, but you will find that it is not going to be easy to deceive us. We are not such fools as the people of Castrum Mare believe us to be."

"Where is this Castrum Mare and what is it?" asked Tarzan.

The officer laughed. "You are very clever," he said.

"I assure you," said the ape-man, "that I am not trying to deceive you. Believe me for a moment and answer one question."

"What is it you wish to ask?"

"Has another white man come into your country within the last few weeks? He is the one for whom I am searching."

"No white man has entered this country," replied the officer, "since Marcus Crispus Sanguinarius led the Third Cohort of the Tenth Legion in victorious conquest of the barbarians who inhabited it eighteen hundred and twenty-three years ago."

"And if a stranger were in your country you would know it?" asked Tarzan.

"If he were in Castra Sanguinarius, yes," replied the officer, "but if he had entered Castrum Mare at the east end of the valley I should not know it; but come, I was not sent here to answer questions, but to fetch you before one who will ask them."

At a word from the officer, the soldiers who accompanied him conducted Tarzan from the dungeon, along the corridor through which he had come the previous day and up into the city. The detachment proceeded for a mile through the city streets to an imposing building, before the entrance to which there was stationed a military guard whose elaborate cuirasses, helmets, and crests suggested that they might be a part of a select military organization.

The metal plates of their cuirasses appeared to Tarzan to be of gold, as did the metal of their helmets, while the hilts and scabbards of their swords were elaborately carved and further ornamented with colored stones ingeniously inlaid in the metal, and to their gorgeous appearance was added the final touch of scarlet cloaks.

The officer who met the party at the gate admitted Tarzan, the interpreter, and the officer who had brought him, but the guard of soldiery was replaced by a detachment of resplendent men-at-arms similar to those who guarded the entrance to the palace.

Tarzan was taken immediately into the building and along a wide corridor, from which opened many chambers, to a large, oblong room flanked by stately columns. At the far end of the apartment a large man sat in a huge, carved chair upon a raised dais.

There were many other people in the room, nearly all of whom were colorfully garbed in bright cloaks over colored tunics and ornate cuirasses of leather or metal, while others wore only simple flowing togas, usually of white. Slaves, messengers, officers were constantly entering or leaving the chamber. The party accompanying Tarzan withdrew between the columns at one side of the room and waited there.

"What is this place?" asked Tarzan of the Bagego interpreter, "and who is the man at the far end of the room?"

"This is the throne-room of the Emperor of the West and that is Sublatus Imperator himself."

For some time Tarzan watched the scene before him with interest. He saw people, evidently of all classes, approach the throne and address the Emperor, and though he could not understand their words, he judged that they were addressing pleas to their ruler. There were patricians among the suppliants, brown-skinned shopkeepers, barbarians resplendent in their savage finery, and even slaves.

The Emperor, Sublatus, presented an imposing figure. Over a tunic of white linen, the Emperor wore a cuirass of gold. His sandals were of white with gold buckles, and from his shoulders fell the purple robe of the Cæsars. A fillet of embroidered linen about his brow was the only other insignia of his station.

Directly behind the throne were heavy hangings against which were ranged a file of soldiers bearing poles surmounted by silver eagles and various other devices, and banners, of the meaning and purpose of which Tarzan was ignorant. Upon every column along the side of the wall were hung shields of various shapes over crossed banners and standards similar to those ranged behind the Emperor. Everything pertaining to the embellishment of the room was martial, the mural decorations being crudely painted scenes of war.

Presently a man, who appeared to be an official of the court, approached them and addressed the officer who had brought Tarzan from the Colosseum.

"Are you Maximus Præclarus?" he demanded.

"Yes," replied the officer.

"Present yourself with the prisoner."

As Tarzan advanced toward the throne surrounded by the detachment of the guard, all eyes were turned upon him, for he was a conspicuous figure even in this assemblage of gorgeously appareled courtiers and soldiers, though his only garments were a loincloth and a leopard skin. His suntanned skin, his shock of black hair, and his gray eyes might not alone have marked him especially in such an assemblage, for there were other dark-skinned, black-haired, gray-eyed men among them, but there was only one who towered inches above them all and he was Tarzan. The undulating smoothness of his easy stride suggested even to the mind of the proud and haughty Sublatus the fierce and savage power of the king of beasts, which perhaps accounted for the fact that the Emperor, with raised hand, halted the party a little further from the throne than usual.

As the party halted before the throne, Tarzan did not wait to be questioned, but, turning to the Bagego interpreter, said: "Ask Sublatus why I have been made a prisoner and tell him that I demand that he free me at once."

The man quailed. "Do as I tell you," said Tarzan.

"What is he saying?" asked Sublatus of the interpreter.

"I fear to repeat such words to the Emperor," replied the man.

"I command it," said Sublatus.

"He asked why he has been made a prisoner and demands that he be released at once."

"Ask him who he is," said Sublatus, angrily, "that he dares issue commands to Sublatus Imperator."

"Tell him," said Tarzan, after the Emperor's words had been translated to him, "that I am Tarzan of the Apes, but if that means as little to him as his name means to me, I have other means to convince him that I am as accustomed to issuing orders and being obeyed as is he."

"Take the insolent dog away," replied Sublatus with trembling voice after he had been told what Tarzan's words had been.

The soldiers laid hold of Tarzan, but he shook them off. "Tell him," snapped the ape-man, "that as one white man to another I demand an answer to my question. Tell him that I did not approach his country as an enemy, but as a friend, and that I shall look to him to see that I am accorded the treatment to which I am entitled, and that before I leave this room."

When these words were translated to Sublatus, the purple of his enraged face matched the imperial purple of his cloak.

"Take him away," he shrieked. "Take him away. Call the guard. Throw Maximus Præclarus into chains for permitting a prisoner to thus address Sublatus."

Two soldiers seized Tarzan, one his right arm, the other his left, but he swung them suddenly together before him and with such force did their heads meet that they relaxed their grasps upon him and sank unconscious to the floor, and then it was that the ape-man leaped with the agility of a cat to the dais where sat the Emperor, Sublatus.

So quickly had the act been accomplished and so unexpected was it that there was none prepared to come between Tarzan and the Emperor in time to prevent the terrible indignity that Tarzan proceeded to inflict upon him.

Seizing the Emperor by the shoulder, he lifted him from his throne and wheeled him about and then grasping him by the scruff of the neck and the bottom of his cuirass, he lifted him from the floor just as several pikemen leaped forward to rescue Sublatus. But when they were about to menace Tarzan with their pikes, he used the body of the screaming Sublatus as a shield so that the soldiers dared not to attack for fear of killing their Emperor.

"Tell them," said Tarzan to the Bagego interpreter, "that if any man interferes with me before I have reached the street, I shall wring the Emperor's neck. Tell him to order them back. If he does, I shall set him free when he is out of the building. If he refuses, it will be at his own risk."

When this message was given to Sublatus, he stopped screaming orders to his people to attack the ape-man and instead warned them to permit Tarzan to leave the palace. Carrying the Emperor above his head, Tarzan leaped from the dais and as he did so the courtiers fell back in accordance with the commands of Sublatus, who now ordered them to turn their backs that they might not witness the indignity that was being done their ruler.

Down the long throne-room and through the corridors to the outer court Tarzan of the Apes carried Sublatus Imperator above his head and at the command of the ape-man the black interpreter went ahead, but there was no need for him, since Sublatus kept the road clear as he issued commands in a voice that trembled with a combination of rage, fear, and mortification.

At the outer gate the members of the guard begged to be permitted to rescue Sublatus and avenge the insult that had been put upon him, but the Emperor warned them to permit his captor to leave the palace in safety, provided he kept his word and liberated Sublatus when they had reached the avenue beyond the gate.

The scarlet-cloaked guard fell back grumbling, their eyes filled with anger because of the humiliation of their Emperor. Even though they had no love for him, yet he was the personification of the power and dignity of their government, and the scene that they witnessed filled them with mortification as the half-naked barbarian bore their commander-in-chief through the palace gates out into the tree-bordered avenue beyond, while the interpreter marched ahead, scarce knowing whether to be more downcast by terror or elated through pride in this unwonted publicity.

The city of Castra Sanguinarius had been carved from the primeval forest that clothed the west end of the canyon, and with unusual vision the founders of the city had cleared only such spaces as were necessary for avenues, buildings, and similar purposes. Ancient trees overhung the avenue before the palace and in many places their foliage overspread the low housetops, mingling with the foliage of the trees in inner courtyards.

Midway of the broad avenue the ape-man halted and lowered Sublatus to the ground. He turned his eyes in the direction of the gateway through which the soldiers of Sublatus were crowding out into the avenue.

"Tell them," said Tarzan to the interpreter, "to go back into the palace grounds; then and then only shall I release their Emperor," for Tarzan had noted the ready javelins in the hands of many of the guardsmen and guessed that the moment his body ceased to be protected by the near presence of Sublatus it would be the target and the goal of a score of the weapons.

When the interpreter deliver the ape-man's ultimatum to them, the guardsmen hesitated, but Sublatus commanded them to obey, for the barbarian's heavy grip upon his shoulder convinced him that there was no hope that he might escape alive or uninjured unless he and his soldiers acceded to the creature's demand. As the last of the guardsmen passed back into the palace courtyard Tarzan released the Emperor and as Sublatus hastened quickly toward the gate, the guardsmen made a sudden sally into the avenue.

They saw their quarry turn and take a few quick steps, leap high into the air and disappear amidst the foliage of an overhanging oak. A dozen javelins hurtled among the branches of the tree. The soldiers rushed forward, their eyes strained upward, but the quarry had vanished.

Sublatus was close upon their heels. "Quick!" he cried. "After him! A thousand denarii to the man who brings down the barbarian."

"There he goes!" cried one, pointing.

"No," cried another. "I saw him there among the foliage. I saw the branches move," and he pointed in the opposite direction.

And in the meantime the ape-man moved swiftly through the trees along one side of the avenue, dropped to a low roof, crossed it and sprang into a tree that rose from an inner court, pausing there to listen for signs of pursuit. After the manner of a wild beast hunted through his native jungle, he moved as silently as the shadow of a shadow, so that now, although he crouched scarce twenty feet above them, the two people in the courtyard below him were unaware of his presence.

But Tarzan was not unaware of theirs and as he listened to the noise of the growing pursuit, that was spreading now in all directions through the city, he took note of the girl and the man in the garden beneath him. It was apparent that the man was wooing the maid, and Tarzan needed no knowledge of their spoken language to interpret the gestures, the glances, and the facial expressions of passionate pleading upon the part of the man or the cold aloofness of the girl.

Sometimes a tilt of her head presented a partial view of her profile to the ape-man and he guessed that she was very beautiful, but the face of the young man with her reminded him of the face of Pamba the rat.

It was evident that his courtship was not progressing to the liking of the youth and now there were evidences of anger in his tone. The girl rose haughtily and with a cold word turned away,. and then the man leaped to his feet from the bench upon which they had been sitting and seized her roughly by the arm. She turned surprised and angry eyes upon him and had half voiced a cry for help when the rat-faced man clapped a hand across her mouth and with his free arm dragged her into his embrace.

Now all this was none of Tarzan's affair. The shes of the city of Castra Sanguinarius meant no more to the savage ape-man than did the shes of the village of Nyuto, chief of the Bagegos. They meant no more to him than did Sabor the lioness and far less than did the shes of the tribe of Akut or of Toyat the king apes—but Tarzan of the Apes was often a creature of impulses; now he realized that he did not like the rat-faced young man, and that he never could like him, while the girl that he was maltreating seemed to be doubly likable because of her evident aversion to her tormentor.

The man had bent the girl's frail body back upon the bench. His lips were close to hers when there was a sudden jarring of the ground beside him and he turned astonished eyes upon the figure of a half-naked giant. Steel-gray eyes looked into his beady black ones, a heavy hand fell upon the collar of his tunic, and he felt himself lifted from the body of the girl and then hurled roughly aside.

He saw his assailant lift his victim to her feet and his little eyes saw, too, another thing: the stranger was unarmed! Then it was that the sword of Fastus leaped from its scabbard and that Tarzan of the Apes found himself facing naked steel. The girl saw what Fastus would do. She saw that the stranger who protected her was unarmed and she leaped between them, at the same time calling loudly, "Axuch! Sarus! Mpingu! Hither! Quickly!"

Tarzan seized the girl and swung her quickly behind him, and simultaneously Fastus was upon him. But the Roman had reckoned without his host and the easy conquest over an unarmed man that he had expected seemed suddenly less easy of accomplishment, for when his keen Spanish sword swung down to cleave the body of his foe, that foe was not there.

Never in his life had Fastus witnessed such agility. It was as though the eyes and body of the barbarian moved more rapidly than the sword of Fastus, and always a fraction of an inch ahead.

Three times Fastus swung viciously at the stranger, and three times his blade cut empty air, while the girl, wide-eyed with astonishment, watched the seemingly unequal duel. Her heart filled with admiration for this strange young giant, who, though he was evidently a barbarian, looked more the patrician than Fastus himself. Three times the blade of Fastus cut harmlessly through empty air—and then there was a lightning-like movement on the part of his antagonist. A brown hand shot beneath the guard of the Roman, steel fingers gripped his wrist, and an instant later his sword clattered to the tile walk of the courtyard. At the same moment two white men and a Negro hurried breathlessly into the garden and ran quickly forward—two with daggers in their hands and one, the black, with a sword.

They saw Tarzan standing between Fastus and the girl. They saw the man in the grip of a stranger. They saw the sword clatter to the ground, and naturally they reached the one conclusion that seemed possible—Fastus was being worsted in an attempt to protect the girl against a stranger.

Tarzan saw them coming toward him and realized that three to one are heavy odds. He was upon the point of using Fastus as a shield against his new enemies when the girl stepped before the three and motioned them to stop. Again the tantalizing tongue that he could almost understand and yet not quite, as the girl explained the circumstances to the newcomers while Tarzan still stood holding Fastus by the wrist.

Presently the girl turned to Tarzan and addressed him, but he only shook his head to indicate that he could not understand her; then, as his eyes fell upon the Negro, a possible means of communicating with these people occurred to him, for the Negro resembled closely the Bagegos of the outer world.

"Are you a Bagego?" asked Tarzan in the language of that tribe.

The man looked surprised. "Yes," he said, "I am, but who are you?"

"And you speak the language of these people?" asked Tarzan, indicating the young woman and Fastus and ignoring the man's query.

"Of course," said the Negro. "I have been a prisoner among them for many years, but there are many Bagegos among my fellow prisoners and we have not forgotten the language of our mothers."

"Good," said Tarzan. "Through you this young woman may speak to me."

"She wants to know who you are, and where you came from, and what you were doing in her garden, and how you got here, and how you happened to protect her from Fastus, and—"

Tarzan held up his hand. "One at a time," he cried. "Tell her I am Tarzan of the Apes, a stranger from a far country, and I came here in friendship seeking one of my own people who is lost."

Now came an interruption in the form of loud pounding and hallooing beyond the outer doorway of the building.

"See what that may be, Axuch," directed the girl, and as the one so addressed, and evidently a slave, humbly turned to do her bidding, she once more addressed Tarzan through the interpreter.

"You have won the gratitude of Dilecta," she said, "and you shall be rewarded by her father."

At this moment Axuch returned followed by a young officer. As the eyes of the newcomer fell upon Tarzan they went wide and he started back, his hand going to the hilt of his sword, and simultaneously Tarzan recognized him as Maximus Præclarus, the young patrician officer who had conducted him from the Colosseum to the palace.

"Lay off your sword, Maximus Præclarus," said the young girl, "for this man is no enemy."

"And you are sure of that, Dilecta?" demanded Præclarus. "What do you know of him?"

"I know that he came in time to save me from this swine who would have harmed me," said the girl haughtily, casting a withering glance at Fastus.

"I do not understand," said Præclarus. "This is a barbarian prisoner of war who calls himself Tarzan and whom I took this morning from the Colosseum to the palace at the command of the Emperor, that Sublatus might look upon the strange creature, whom some thought to be a spy from Castrum Mare."

"If he is a prisoner, what is he doing here, then?" demanded the girl. "And why are you here?"

"This fellow attacked the Emperor himself and then escaped from the palace. The entire city is being searched and I, being in charge of a detachment of soldiers assigned to this district, came immediately hither, fearing the very thing that has happened and that this wild man might find you and do you harm."

"It was the patrician, Fastus, son of Imperial Cæsar, who

would have harmed me," said the girl. "It was the wild man who saved me from him."

Maximum Præclarus looked quickly at Fastus, the son of Sublatus, and then at Tarzan. The young officer appeared to be resting upon the horns of a dilemma.

"There is your man," said Fastus, with a sneer. "Back to the dungeons with him."

"Maximus Præclarus does not take orders from Fastus," said the young man, "and he knows his duty without consulting him."

"You will arrest this man who has protected me, Præclarus?" demanded Dilecta.

"What else may I do?" asked Præclarus. "It is my duty."

"Then do it," sneered Fastus.

Præclarus went white. "It is with difficulty that I can keep my hands off you, Fastus," he said. "If you were the son of Jupiter himself, it would not take much more to get yourself choked. If you know what is well for you, you will go before I lose control of my temper."

"Mpingu," said Dilecta, "show Fastus to the avenue."

Fastus flushed. "My father, the Emperor, shall hear of this," he snarled; "and do not forget, Dilecta, your father stands none too well in the estimation of Sublatus Imperator."

"Get gone," cried Dilecta, "before I order my slave to throw you into the avenue."

With a sneer and a swagger Fastus quit the garden, and when he had gone Dilecta turned to Maximus Præclarus.

"What shall we do?" she cried. "I must protect this noble stranger who saved me from Fastus, and at the same time you must do your duty and return him to Sublatus."

"I have a plan," said Maximus Præclarus, "but I cannot carry it out unless I can talk with the stranger."

"Mpingu can understand and interpret for him," said the girl.

"Can you trust Mpingu implicitly?" asked Præclarus.

"Absolutely," said Dilecta.

"Then send away the others," said Præclarus, indicating Axuch and Sarus; and when Mpingu returned from escorting Fastus to the street he found Maximus Præclarus, Dilecta, and Tarzan alone in the garden.

Præclarus motioned Mpingu to advance. "Tell the stranger that I have been sent to arrest him," he said to Mpingu, "but tell him also that because of the service he has rendered Dilecta I wish to protect him, if he will follow my instructions."

"What are they?" asked Tarzan when the question had been put to him. "What do you wish me to do?"

70

"I wish you to come with me," said Præclarus; "to come with me as though you are my prisoner. I shall take you in the direction of the Colosseum and when I am opposite my own home I shall give you a signal so that you will understand that the house is mine. Immediately afterward I will make it possible for you to escape into the trees as you did when you quit the palace with Sublatus. Go, then, immediately to my house and remain there until I return. Dilecta will send Mpingu there now to warn my servants that you are coming. At my command they will protect you with their lives. Do you understand?"

"I understand," replied the ape-man, when the plan had been explained to him by Mpingu.

"Later," said Præclarus, "we may be able to find a way to get you out of Castra Sanguinarius and across the mountains."

10

THE cares of state rested lightly upon the shoulders of Validus Augustus, Emperor of the East, for though his title was imposing his domain was small and his subjects few. The island city of Castrum Mare boasted a population of only a trifle more than twenty-two thousand people, of which some three thousand were whites and nineteen thousand of mixed blood, while outside the city, in the villages of the lake dwellers and along the eastern shore of Mare Orientis, dwelt the balance of his subjects, comprising some twenty-six thousand Negroes.

Today, reports and audiences disposed of, the Emperor had withdrawn to the palace garden to spend an hour in conversation with a few of his intimates, while his musicians, concealed within a vine-covered bower, entertained him. While he was thus occupied a chamberlain approached and announced that the patrician Fulvus Fupus begged an audience of the Emperor.

"Fulvus knows that the audience hour is past," snapped the Emperor. "Bid him come on the morrow."

"He insists, most glorious Cæsar," said the chamberlain, "that his business is of the utmost importance and that it is

71

only because he felt that the safety of the Emperor is at stake that he came at this hour."

"Bring him here then," commanded Validus, and, as the chamberlain turned away, "Am I never to have a moment's relaxation without some fool like Fulvus Fupus breaking in upon me with some silly story?" he grumbled to one of his companions.

When Fulvus approached the Emperor a moment later, he was received with a cold and haughty stare.

"I have come, most glorious Cæsar," said Fulvus, "to fulfill the duty of a citizen of Rome, whose first concern should be the safety of his Emperor."

"What are you talking about?" snapped Validus. "Quick, out with it!"

"There is a stranger in Castrum Mare who claims to be a barbarian from Germania, but I believe him to be a spy from Castrum Sanguinarius where, it is said, Cassius Hasta is an honored guest of Sublatus, in that city."

"What do you know about Cassius Hasta and what has he to do with it?" demanded Validus.

"It is said—it is rumored," stammered Fulvus Fupus, "that—"

"I have heard too many rumors already about Cassius Hasta," exclaimed Validus. "Can I not dispatch my nephew upon a mission without every fool in Castrum Mare lying awake nights to conjure motives, which may later be ascribed to me?"

"It is only what I heard," said Fulvus, flushed and uncomfortable. "I do not know anything about it. I did not say that I knew."

"Well, what did you hear?" demanded Validus. "Come, out with it."

"The talk is common in the Baths that you sent Cassius Hasta away because he was plotting treason and that he went at once to Sublatus, who received him in a friendly fashion and that together they are planning an attack upon Castrum Mare."

Validus scowled. "Baseless rumor," he said; "but what about this prisoner? What has he to do with it and why have I not been advised of his presence?"

"That I do not know," said Fulvus Fupus. "That is why I felt it doubly my duty to inform you, since the man who is harboring the stranger is a most powerful patrician and one who might well be ambitious."

"Who is he?" asked the Emperor.

"Septimus Favonius," replied Fupus.

"Septimus Favonius!" exclaimed Validus. "Impossible."

"Not so impossible," said Fupus, boldly, "if glorious

Cæsar will but recall the friendship that ever existed between Cassius Hasta and Mallius Lepus, the nephew of Septimus Favonius. The home of Septimus Favonius was the other home of Cassius Hasta. To whom, then, sooner might he turn for aid than to this powerful friend whose ambitions are well known outside the palace, even though they may not as yet have come to the ears of Validus Augustus?"

Nervously the Emperor arose and paced to and fro, the eyes of the others watching him narrowly; those of Fulvus Fupus narrowed with malign anticipation.

Presently Validus halted and turned toward one of his courtiers. "May Hercules strike me dead," he cried, "if there be not some truth in what Fulvus Fupus suggests!" and to Fupus, "What is this stranger like?"

"He is a man of white skin, yet of slightly different complexion and appearance than the usual patrician. He feigns to speak our language with a certain practiced stiltedness that is intended to suggest lack of familiarity. This, I think, is merely a part of the ruse to deceive."

"How did he come into Castrum Mare and none of my officers report the matter to me?" asked Validus.

"That you may learn from Mallius Lepus," said Fulvus Fupus, "for Mallius Lepus was in command of the Porta Decumana when some of the barbarians of the lake villages brought him there, presumably a prisoner, yet Cæsar knows how easy it would have been to bribe these creatures to play such a part."

"You explain it so well, Fulvus Fupus," said the Emperor, "that one might even suspect you to have been the instigator of the plot, or at least to have given much thought to similar schemes."

"Cæsar's ever brilliant wit never deserts him," said Fupus, forcing a smile, though his face paled.

"We shall see," snapped Validus, and turning to one of his officers, "Order the arrest of Septimus Favonius, and Mallius Lepus and this stranger at once."

As he ceased speaking a chamberlain entered the garden and approached the Emperor. "Septimus Favonius requests an audience," he announced. "Mallius Lepus, his nephew, and a stranger are with him."

"Fetch them," said Validus, and to the officer who was about to depart to arrest them, "Wait here. We shall see what Septimus Favonius has to say."

A moment later the three entered and approached the Emperor. Favonius and Lepus saluted Validus and then the former presented von Harben as a barbarian chief from Germania.

"We have already heard of this barbarian chief," said

Validus, with a sneer. Favonius and Lepus glanced at Fupus. "Why was I not immediately notified of the capture of this prisoner?" This time the Emperor directed his remarks to Mallius Lepus.

"There has been little delay, Cæsar," replied the young officer. "It was necessary that he be bathed and properly clothed before he was brought here."

"It was not necessary that he be brought here," said Validus. "There are dungeons in Castrum Mare for prisoners from Castra Sanguinarius."

"He is not from Castra Sanguinarius," said Septimus Favonius.

"Where are you from and what are you doing in my country?" demanded Validus, turning upon von Harben.

"I am from a country that your historians knew as Germania," replied Erich.

"And I suppose you learned to speak our language in Germania," sneered Validus.

"Yes," replied von Harben, "I did."

"And you have never been to Castra Sanguinarius?" "Never."

"I presume you have been to Rome," laughed Validus.

"Yes, many times," replied von Harben.

"And who is Emperor there now?"

"There is no Roman Emperor," said von Harben.

"No Roman Emperor!" exclaimed Validus. "If you are not a spy from Castra Sanguinarius, you are a lunatic. Perhaps you are both, for no one but a lunatic would expect me to believe such a story. No Roman Emperor, indeed!"

"There is no Roman Emperor," said von Harben, "because there is no Roman Empire. Mallius Lepus tells me that your country has had no intercourse with the outside world for more than eighteen hundred years. Much can happen in that time—much has happened. Rome fell, over a thousand years ago. No nation speaks its language today, which is understood by priests and scholars only. The barbarians of Germania, of Gallia, and of Britannia have built empires and civilizations of tremendous power, and Rome is only a city in Italia."

Mallius Lepus was beaming delightedly. "I told you," he whispered to Favonius, "that you would love him. By Jupiter, I wish he would tell Validus the story of the litters that travel fifty thousand paces an hour!"

There was that in the tone and manner of von Harben that compelled confidence and belief, so that even the suspicious Validus gave credence to the seemingly wild tales of the stranger and presently found himself asking questions of the barbarian.

Finally the Emperor turned to Fulvus Fupus. "Upon what proof did you accuse this man of being a spy from Castra Sanguinarius?" he demanded.

"Where else may he be from?" asked Fulvus Fupus. "We know he is not from Castrum Mare, so he must be from Castra Sanguinarius."

"You have no evidence then to substantiate your accusations?"

Fupus hesitated.

"Get out," ordered Validus, angrily. "I shall attend to you later."

Overcome by mortification, Fupus left the garden, but the malevolent glances that he shot at Favonius, Lepus, and Erich boded them no good. Validus looked long and searchingly at von Harben for several minutes after Fupus quit the garden as though attempting to read the soul of the stranger standing before him.

"So there is no Emperor at Rome," he mused, half aloud. "When Sanguinarius led his cohort out of Ægyptus, Nerva was Emperor. That was upon the sixth day before the calends of February in the 848th year of the city in the second year of Nerva's reign. Since that day no word of Rome has reached the descendants of Sanguinarius and his cohort."

Von Harben figured rapidly, searching his memory for the historical dates and data of ancient history that were as fresh in his mind as those of his own day. "The sixth day before the calends of February," he repeated; "that would be the twenty-seventh day of January in the 848th year of the city—why, January twenty-seventh, A.D. 98, is the date of Nerva's death," he said.

"Ah, if Sanguinarius had but known," said Validus, "but Ægyptus is a long way from Rome and Sanguinarius was far to the south up the Nilus before word could have reached his post by ancient Thebæ that his enemy was dead. And who became Emperor after Nerva? Do you know that?"

"Trajan," replied von Harben.

"Why do you, a barbarian, know so much concerning the history of Rome?" asked the Emperor.

"I am a student of such things," replied von Harben. "It has been my ambition to become an authority on the subject."

"Could you write down these happenings since the death of Nerva?"

"I could put down all that I could recall, or all that I have read," said von Harben, "but it would take a long time."

"You shall do it," said Validus, "and you shall have the time."

"But I had not planned remaining on in your country," dissented von Harben.

"You shall remain," said Validus. "You shall also write a history of the reign of Validus Augustus, Emperor of the East."

"But—" interjected von Harben.

"Enough!" snapped Validus. "I am Cæsar. It is a command."

Von Harben shrugged and smiled. Rome and the Cæsars, he realized, had never seemed other than musty parchment and weather-worn inscriptions cut in crumbling stone, until now.

Here, indeed, was a real Cæsar. What matter it that his empire was naught but a few square miles of marsh, an island and swampy shore-land in the bottom of an unknown canyon, or that his subjects numbered less than fifty thousand souls—the first Augustus himself was no more a Cæsar than was his namesake, Validus.

"Come," said Validus, "I shall take you to the library myself, for that will be the scene of your labors."

In the library, which was a vault-like room at the end of a long corridor, Validus displayed with pride several hundred parchment rolls neatly arranged upon shelves.

"Here," said Validus, selecting one of the rolls, "is the story of Sanguinarius and the history of our country up to the founding of Castrum Mare. Take it with you and read it at your leisure, for while you shall remain with Septimus Favonius, whom with Mallius Lepus I shall hold responsible for you, every day you shall come to the palace and I shall dictate to you the history of my rein. Go, now, with Septimus Favonius and at this hour tomorrow attend again upon Cæsar."

When they were outside the palace of Validus Augustus, von Harben turned to Mallius Lepus. "It is a question whether I am prisoner or guest," he said, with a rueful smile.

"Perhaps you are both," said Mallius Lepus, "but that you are even partially a guest is fortunate for you. Validus Augustus is vain, arrogant, and cruel. He is also suspicious, for he knows that he is not popular, and Fulvus Fupus had evidently almost succeeded in bringing your doom upon you and ruin to Favonius and myself before we arrived. What strange whim altered the mind of Cæsar I do not know, but it is fortunate for you that it was altered; fortunate, too, for Septimus Favonius and Mallius Lepus."

"But it will take years to write the history of Rome," said von Harben.

"And if you refuse to write it you will be dead many more years than it would take to accomplish the task," retorted Mallius Lepus, with a grin.

"Castrum Mare is not an unpleasant place in which to live," said Septimus Favonius.

"Perhaps you are right," said von Harben, as the face of the daughter of Favonius presented itself to his mind.

Returned to the home of the host, the instinct of the archæologist and the scholar urged von Harben to an early perusal of the ancient papyrus roll that Cæsar had loaned him, so that no sooner was he in the apartments that had been set aside for him than he stretched himself upon a long sofa and untied the cords that confined the roll.

As it unrolled before his eyes he saw a manuscript in ancient Latin, marred by changes and erasures, yellowed by age. It was quite unlike anything that had previously fallen into his hands during his scholary investigations into the history and literature of ancient Rome. For whereas such other original ancient manuscripts as he had had the good fortune to examine had been the work of clerks or scholars, a moment's glance at this marked it as the laborious effort of a soldier unskilled in literary pursuits.

The manuscript bristled with the rough idiom of far-flung camps of veteran legionaries, with the slang of Rome and Egypt of nearly two thousand years before, and there were references to people and places that appeared in no histories or geographies known to modern man—little places and little people that were without fame in their own time and whose very memory had long since been erased from the consciousness of man, but yet in this crude manuscript they lived again for Erich von Harben—the quæstor who had saved the life of Sanguinarius in an Egyptian town that never was on any map, and there was Marcus Crispus Sanguinarius himself who had been of sufficient importance to win the enmity of Nerva in the year 90 A.D. while the latter was consul—Marcus Crispus Sanguinarius, the founder of an empire, whose name appears nowhere in the annals of ancient Rome.

With mounting interest von Harben read the complaints of Sanguinarius and his anger because the enmity of Nerva had caused him to be relegated to the hot sands of this distant post below the ancient city of Thebæ in far Ægyptus.

Writing in the third person, Sanguinarius had said:

"Sanguinarius, a præfect of the Third Cohort of the Tenth Legion, stationed below Thebæ in Ægyptus in the 846th year of the city, immediately after Nerva assumed the purple, was accused of having plotted against the Emperor.

"About the fifth day before the calends of February in the 848th year of the city a messenger came to Sanguinarius from Nerva commanding the præfect to return to Rome and place himself under arrest, but this Sanguinarius had no mind to do, and as no other in his camp knew the nature of the message he had received from Nerva, Sanguinarius struck the messenger down with his dagger and caused the word to be spread among his men that the man had been an assassin sent from Rome and that Sanguinarius had slain him in self-defense.

"He also told his lieutenants and centurions that Nerva was sending a large force to destroy the cohort and he prevailed upon them to follow up the Nilus in search of a new country where they might establish themselves far from the malignant power of a jealous Cæsar, and upon the following day the long march commenced.

"It so happened that shortly before this a fleet of one hundred and twenty vessels landed at Myos-hormos, a port of Ægyptus on the Sinus Arabius. This merchant fleet annually brought rich merchandise from the island of Taprobana—silk, the value of which was equal to its weight in gold, pearls, diamonds, and a variety of aromatics and other merchandise, which was transferred to the backs of camels and brought inland from Myos-hormos to the Nilus and down that river to Alexandria, whence it was shipped to Rome.

"With this caravan were hundreds of slaves from India and far Cathay and even light-skinned people captured in the distant northwest by Mongol raiders. The majority of these were young girls destined for the auction block at Rome. And it so chanced that Sanguinarius met this caravan, heavy with riches and women, and captured it. During the ensuing five years the cohort settled several times in what they hoped would prove a permanent camp, but it was not until the 853rd year of Rome that, by accident, they discovered the hidden canyon where now stands Castra Sanguinarius."

"You find it interesting?" inquired a voice from the doorway, and looking up von Harben saw Mallius Lepus standing on the threshold.

"Very," said Erich.

Lepus shrugged his shoulders. "We suspect that it would have been more interesting had the old assassin written the truth," said Lepus. "As a matter of fact, very little is known concerning his reign, which lasted for twenty years. He was assassinated in the year 20 Anno Sanguinarii, which corresponds to the 873rd year of Rome. The old buck named the city after himself, decreed a calendar of his own, and had his head stamped on gold coins, many of which are still in existence. Even today we use his calendar quite as much as that of our Roman ancestors, but in Castrum Mare we have tried to forget the example of Sanguinarius as much as possible."

"What is this other city that I have heard mentioned so

often and that is called Castra Sanguinarius?" asked von Harben.

"It is the original city founded by Sanguinarius," replied Lepus. "For a hundred years after the founding of the city conditions grew more and more intolerable until no man's life or property was safe, unless he was willing to reduce himself almost to the status of a slave and continually fawn upon the Emperor. It was then that Honus Hasta revolted and led a few hundred families to this island at the eastern end of the valley, founding the city and the empire of Castrum Mare. Here, for over seventeen hundred years, the descendants of these families have lived in comparative peace and security, but in an almost constant state of war with Castra Sanguinarius.

"From mutual necessity the two cities carry on a commerce that is often interrupted by raids and wars. The suspicion and hatred that the inhabitants of each city feel for the inhabitants of the other is fostered always by our Emperors, each of whom fears that friendly communication between the two cities would result in the overthrow of one of them."

"And now Castrum Mare is happy and contented under Cæsar?" asked Erich.

"That is a question that it might not be safe to answer honestly," said Lepus, with a shrug.

"If I am going to the palace every day to write the history of Rome for Validus Augustus and receive from him the story of his reign," said von Harben, "it might be well if I knew something of the man, otherwise there is a chance for me to get into serious trouble, which might conceivably react upon you and Septimus Favonius, whom Cæsar has made responsible for me. If you care to forewarn me, I promise you that I shall repeat nothing that you may tell me."

Lepus, leaning lightly against the wall by the doorway, played idly with the hilt of his dagger as he took thought before replying. Presently he looked up, straight into von Harben's eyes.

"I shall trust you," he said; "first, because there is that in you which inspires confidence, and, second, because it cannot profit you to harm either Septimus Favonius or myself. Castrum Mare is not happy with its Cæsar. He is arrogant and cruel—not like the Cæsars to which Castrum Mare has been accustomed.

"The last Emperor was a kindly man, but at the time of his death his brother, Validus Augustus, was chosen to succeed him because Cæsar's son was, at that time, but a year old.

"This son of the former Emperor, a nephew of Validus

Augustus, is called Cassius Hasta. And because of his popularity he has aroused the jealousy and hatred of Augustus, who recently sent him away upon a dangerous mission to the west end of the valley. There are many who consider it virtual banishment, but Validus Augustus insists that this is not the fact. No one knows what Cassius Hasta's orders were. He went secretly by night and was accompanied by only a few slaves.

"It is believed that he has been ordered to enter Castra Sanguinarius as a spy, and if such is the case his mission amounts practically to a sentence of death. If this were known for a fact, the people would rise against Validus Augustus, for Cassius Hasta was the most popular man in Castrum Mare.

"But enough. I shall not bore you with the sorrows of Castrum Mare. Take your reading down into the garden where in the shade of the trees, it is cooler than here and I shall join you presently."

As von Harben lay stretched upon the sward beneath the shade of a tree in the cool garden of Septimus Favonius, his mind was not upon the history of Sanguinarius, nor upon the political woes of Castrum Mare so much as they were upon plans for escape.

As a scholar, an explorer, and an archæologist he would delight in remaining here for such a time as might be necessary for him to make an exploration of the valley and study the government and customs of its inhabitants, but to remain cooped up in the vault-like library of the Emperor of the East writing the history of ancient Rome in Latin with a reed pen on papyrus rolls in no way appealed to him.

The rustle of fresh linen and the soft fall of sandaled feet upon the graveled garden walk interrupted his trend of thought and as he looked up into the face of Favonia, daughter of Septimus Favonius, the history of ancient Rome together with half-formulated plans for escape were dissipated from his mind by the girl's sweet smile, as is a morning mist by the rising sun.

11

As Maximus Præclarus led Tarzan of the Apes from the home of Dion Splendidus in the city of Castra Sanguinarius, the soldiers, gathered by the doorway, voiced their satisfaction in oaths and exclamations. They liked the young patrician who commanded them and they were proud that he should have captured the wild barbarian single-handed.

A command from Præclarus brought silence and at a word from him they formed around the prisoner, and the march toward the Colosseum was begun. They had proceeded but a short distance when Præclarus halted the detachment and went himself to the doorway of a house fronting on the avenue through which they were crossing. He halted before the door, stood in thought for a moment, and then turned back toward his detachment as though he had changed his mind about entering, and Tarzan knew that the young officer was indicating to him the home in which he lived and in which the ape-man might find sanctuary later.

Several hundred yards farther along the street, after they had resumed the march, Præclarus halted his detachment beneath the shade of great trees opposite a drinking fountain, which was built into the outside of a garden wall close beside an unusually large tree, which, overspreading the avenue upon one side and the wall on the other, intermingled its branches with those of other trees growing inside the garden beyond.

Præclarus crossed the avenue and drank at the fountain and returning inquired by means of signs if Tarzan would drink. The ape-man nodded in assent and Præclarus gave orders that he be permitted to cross to the fountain.

Slowly Tarzan walked to the other side of the avenue. He stooped and drank from the fountain. Beside him was the bole of a great tree; above him was the leafy foliage that would conceal him from the sight and protect him from the missiles of the soldiers. Turning from the fountain, a quick step took him behind the tree. One of the soldiers shouted a warning to Præclarus, and the whole detachment, immediately suspicious, leaped quickly across the avenue, led by the young patrician who commanded them, but when they reached the fountain and the tree their prisoner had vanished.

Shouting their disappointment, they gazed upward into the foliage, but there was no sign there of the barbarian. Several of the more active soldiers scrambled into the branches and then Maximus Præclarus, pointing in the direction opposite to that in which his home lay, shouted: "This way, there he goes!" and started on a run down the avenue, while behind him strung his detachment, their pikes ready in their hands.

Moving silently through the branches of the great trees that overhung the greater part of the city of Castra Sanguinarius, Tarzan paralleled the avenue leading back to the home of Maximus Præclarus, halting at last in a tree that

81

overlooked the inner courtyard or walled garden, which appeared to be a distinguishing feature of the architecture of the city.

Below him he saw a matronly woman of the patrician class, listening to a tall Negro who was addressing her excitedly. Clustered about the woman and eagerly listening to the words of the speaker were a number of slaves, both men and women.

Tarzan recognized the speaker as Mpingu, and, though he could not understand his words, realized that the man was preparing them for his arrival in accordance with the instructions given him in the garden of Dion Splendidus by Maximus Præclarus, and that he was making a good story of it was evidenced by his excited gesticulation and the wide eyes and open mouths of the listening men.

The woman, listening attentively and with quiet dignity of mien, appeared to be slightly amused, but whether at the story itself or at the unrestrained excitement of Mpingu, Tarzan did not know.

She was a regal-looking woman of about fifty, with graying hair and with the poise and manner of that perfect self-assurance which is the hallmark of assured position; that she was a patrician to her finger tips was evident, and yet there was that in her eyes and the little wrinkles at their corners that bespoke a broad humanity and a kindly disposition.

Mpingu had evidently reached the point where his vocabulary could furnish no adequate superlatives wherewith to describe the barbarian who had rescued his mistress from Fastus, and he was acting out in exaggerated pantomime the scene in the garden of his mistress, when Tarzan dropped lightly to the sward beside him. The effect upon the Negroes of this unexpected appearance verged upon the ludicrous, but the white woman was unmoved to any outward sign of surprise.

"Is this the barbarian?" she asked of Mpingu.

"It is he," replied the black.

"Tell him that I am Festivitas, the mother of Maximus Præclarus," the woman directed Mpingu, "and that I welcome him here in the name of my son."

Through Mpingu, Tarzan acknowledged the greetings of Festivitas and thanked her for her hospitality, after which she instructed one of her slaves to conduct the stranger to the apartments that were placed at his disposal.

It was late afternoon before Maximus Præclarus returned to his home, going immediately to Tarzan's apartments. With him was the same man who had acted as interpreter in the morning.

"I am to remain here with you," said the man to Tarzan, "as your interpreter and servant."

"I venture to say," said Præclarus through the interpreter, "that this is the only spot in Castra Sanguinarius that they have not searched for you and there are three centuries combing the forests outside the city, though by this time Sublatus is convinced that you have escaped. We shall keep you here in hiding for a few days when, I think, I can find the means to get you out of the city after dark."

The ape-man smiled. "I can leave whenever I choose," he said, "either by day or by night, but I do not choose to leave until I have satisfied myself that the man for whom I am searching is not here. But, first, let me thank you for your kindness to me, the reason for which I cannot understand."

"That is easily explained," said Præclarus. "The young woman whom you saved from attack this morning is Dilecta, the daughter of Dion Splendidus. She and I are to be married. That, I think, will explain my gratitude."

"I understand," said Tarzan, "and I am glad that I was fortunate enough to come upon them at the time that I did."

"Should you be captured again, it will not prove so fortunate for you," said Præclarus, "for the man from whom you saved Dilecta is Fastus, the son of Sublatus, and now the Emperor will have two indignities to avenge; but if you remain here you will be safe, for our slaves are loyal and there is little likelihood that you will be discovered."

"If I remain here," said Tarzan, "and it should be discovered that you had befriended me, would not the anger of the Emperor fall upon you?"

Maximus Præclarus shrugged. "I am daily expecting that," he said; "not because of you, but because the son of the Emperor wishes to marry Dilecta. Sublatus needs no further excuse to destroy me. I should be no worse off were he to learn that I have befriended you than I now am."

"Then, perhaps, I may be of service to you if I remain," said Tarzan.

"I do not see how you can do anything but remain," said Præclarus. "Every man, woman, and child in Castra Sanguinarius will be on the lookout for you, for Sublatus has offered a huge reward for your capture, and besides the inhabitants of the city there are thousands of barbarians outside the walls who will lay aside every other interest to run you down."

"Twice today you have seen how easily I can escape from the soldiers of Sublatus," said Tarzan, smiling. "Just as easily can I leave the city and elude the barbarians in the outer villages."

"Then why do you remain?" demanded Præclarus.

"I came here searching for the son of a friend," replied Tarzan. "Many weeks ago the young man started out with an expedition to explore the Wiramwazi Mountains in which your country is located. His people deserted him upon the outer slopes, and I am convinced that he is somewhere within the range and very possibly in this canyon. If he is here and alive, he will unquestionably come sooner or later to your city where, from the experience that I have gained, I am sure that he will receive anything but friendly treatment from your Emperor. This is the reason that I wish to remain somewhere in the vicinity, and now that you have told me that you are in danger, I may as well remain in your home where it is possible I may have an opportunity to reciprocate your kindness to me."

"If the son of your friend is in this end of the valley, he will be captured and brought to Castra Sanguinarius," said Maximus Præclarus, "and when that occurs I shall know of it, since I am detailed to duty at the Colosseum—a mark of the disfavor of Sublatus, since this is the most distasteful duty to which an officer can be assigned."

"Is it possible that this man for whom I am searching might be in some other part of the valley?" asked Tarzan.

"No," replied Præclarus. "There is only one entrance to the valley, that through which you were brought, and while there is another city at the eastern end, he could not reach it without passing through the forest surrounding Castra Sanguinarius, in which event he would have been captured by the barbarians and turned over to Sublatus."

"Then I shall remain here," said Tarzan, "for a time."

"You shall be a welcome guest," replied Præclarus.

For three weeks Tarzan remained in the home of Maximus Præclarus. Festivitas conceived a great liking for the bronzed barbarian, and soon tiring of carrying on conversation with him through an interpreter, she set about teaching him her own language, with the result that it was not long before Tarzan could carry on a conversation in Latin; nor did he lack opportunity to practice his new accomplishment, since Festivitas never tired of hearing stories of the outer world and of the manners and customs of modern civilization.

And while Tarzan of the Apes waited in Castra Sanguinarius for word that von Harben had been seen in the valley, the man he sought was living the life of a young patrician attached to the court of the Emperor of the East, and though much of his time was pleasantly employed in the palace library, yet he chafed at the knowledge that he was virtually a prisoner and was often formulating plans for escape—plans that were sometimes forgotten when he sat beneath the spell of the daughter of Septimus Favonius.

And often in the library he discovered only unadulterated pleasure in his work, and thoughts of escape were driven from his mind by discoveries of such gems as original Latin translations of Homer and of hitherto unknown manuscripts of Vergil, Cicero, and Cæsar—manuscripts that dated from the days of the young republic and on down the centuries to include one of the early satires of Juvenal.

Thus the days passed, while far off in another world a frightened little monkey scampered through the upper terraces of a distant forest.

12

A PENCHANT for boasting is not the prerogative of any time, or race, or individual, but is more or less common to all. So it is not strange that Mpingu, filled with the importance of the secret that he alone shared with his mistress and the household of Maximus Præclarus, should have occasionally dropped a word here and there that might impress his listeners with his importance.

Mpingu meant no harm. He was loyal to the house of Dion Splendidus and he would not willingly have brought harm to his master or his master's friend, but so it is often with people who talk too much, and Mpingu certainly had done that. The result was that upon a certain day, as he was bartering in the market-place for provisions for the kitchen of Dion Splendidus, he felt a heavy hand laid upon his shoulder and, turning, he was astonished to find himself looking into the face of a centurion of the palace guard, behind whom stood a file of legionaries.

"You are Mpingu, the slave of Dion Splendidus?" demanded the centurion.

"I am," replied the man.

"Come with us," commanded the centurion.

Mpingu drew back, afraid, as all men feared the soldiers of Cæsar. "What do you want of me?" he demanded. "I have done nothing."

"Come, barbarian," ordered the soldier. "I was not sent to confer with you, but to get you!" And he jerked Mpingu roughly toward him and pushed him back among the soldiers.

A crowd had gathered, as crowds gathered always when a man is arrested, but the centurion ignored the crowd as though it did not exist, and the people fell aside as the soldiers marched away with Mpingu. No one questioned or interfered, for who would dare question an officer of Cæsar? Who would interfere in behalf of a slave?

Mpingu thought that he would be taken to the dungeons beneath the Colosseum, which was the common jail in which all prisoners were confined; but presently he realized that his captors were not leading him in that direction, and when finally it dawned upon him that the palace was their goal he was filled with terror.

Never before had Mpingu stepped foot within the precincts of the palace grounds, and when the imperial gate closed behind him he was in a mental state bordering upon collapse. He had heard stories of the cruelty of Sublatus, of the terrible vengeance wreaked upon his enemies, and he had visions that paralyzed his mind so that he was in a state of semi-consciousness when he was finally led into an inner chamber where a high dignitary of the court confronted him.

"This," said the centurion, who had brought him, "is Mpingu, the slave of Dion Splendidus, whom I was commanded to fetch to you."

"Good!" said the official. "You and your detachment may remain while I question him." Then he turned upon Mpingu. "Do you know the penalties one incurs for aiding the enemies of Cæsar?" he demanded.

Mpingu's lower jaw moved convulsively as though he would reply, but he was unable to control his voice.

"They die," growled the officer, menacingly. "They die terrible deaths that they will remember through all eternity."

"I have done nothing," cried Mpingu, suddenly regaining control of his vocal cords.

"Do not lie to me, barbarian," snapped the official. "You aided in the escape of the prisoner who called himself Tarzan and even now you are hiding him from your Emperor."

"I did not help him escape. I am not hiding him," wailed Mpingu.

"You lie. You know where he is. You boasted of it to other slaves. Tell me where he is."

"I do not know," said Mpingu.

"If your tongue were cut out, you could not tell us where he is," said the Roman. "If red-hot irons were thrust into your eyes, you could not see to lead us to his hiding-place; but if we find him without your help, and we surely shall find him, we shall need neither your tongue nor your eyes. Do you understand?"

"I do not know where he is," repeated Mpingu.

The Roman turned away and struck a single blow upon a gong, after which he stood in silence until a slave entered the room in response to the summons. "Fetch tongs," the Roman instructed the slave, "and a charcoal brazier with burning-irons. Be quick."

After the slave had left, silence fell again upon the apartment. The official was giving Mpingu an opportunity to think, and Mpingu so occupied the time in thinking that it seemed to him that the slave had scarcely left the apartment before he returned again with tongs and a lighted burner, from the glowing heart of which protruded the handle of a burning-iron.

"Have your soldiers throw him to the floor and hold him," said the official to the centurion.

It was evident to Mpingu that the end had come; the officer was not even going to give him another opportunity to speak.

"Wait!" he shrieked.

"Well," said the official, "you are regaining your memory?"

"I am only a slave," wailed Mpingu. "I must do what my masters command."

"And what did they command?" inquired the Roman.

"I was only an interpreter," said Mpingu. "The white barbarian spoke the language of the Bagegos, who are my people. Through me they talked to him and he talked to them."

"And what was said?" demanded the inquisitor.

Mpingu hesitated, dropping his eyes to the floor.

"Come, quickly!" snapped the other.

"I have forgotten," said Mpingu.

The official nodded to the centurion. The soldiers seized Mpingu and threw him roughly to the floor, four of them holding him there, one seated upon each limb.

"The tongs!" directed the official, and the slave handed the instrument to the centurion.

"Wait!" screamed Mpingu. "I will tell you."

"Let him up," said the official; and to Mpingu: "This is your last chance. If you go down again, your tongue comes out and your eyes, too."

"I will talk," said Mpingu. "I did but interpret, that is all. I had nothing to do with helping him to escape or hiding him."

"If you tell us the truth, you will not be punished," said the Roman. "Where is the white barbarian?"

"He is hiding in the home of Maximus Præclarus," said Mpingu.

"What has your master to do with this?" commanded the Romans.

"Dion Splendidus has nothing to do with it," replied Mpingu. "Maximus Præclarus planned it."

"That is all," said the official to the centurion. "Take him away and keep him under guard until you receive further orders. Be sure that he talks to no one."

A few minutes later the official who had interrogated Mpingu entered the apartment of Sablatus while the Emperor was in conversation with his son Fastus.

"I have located the white barbarian, Sublatus," announced the official.

"Good!" said the Emperor. "Where is he?"

"In the home of Maximus Præclarus."

"I might have suspected as much," said Fastus.

"Who else is implicated?" asked Sublatus.

"He was caught in the courtyard of Dion Splendidus," said Fastus, "and the Emperor has heard, as we all have, that Dion Splendidus has long had eyes upon the imperial purple of the Cæsars."

"The slave says that only Maximus Præclarus is responsible for the escape of the barbarian," said the official.

"He was one of Dion Splendidus's slaves, was he not?" demanded Fastus.

"Yes."

"Then it is not strange that he would protect his master," said Fastus.

"Arrest them all," commanded Sublatus.

"You mean Dion Splendidus, Maximus Præclarus, and the barbarian Tarzan?" asked the official.

"I mean those three and the entire household of Dion Splendidus and Maximus Præclarus," replied Sublatus.

"Wait, Cæsar," suggested Fastus; "twice already has the barbarian escaped from the legionaries. If he receives the slightest inkling of this, he will escape again. I have a plan. Listen!"

An hour later a messenger arrived at the home of Dion Splendidus carrying an invitation to the senator and his wife to be the guests of a high court functionary that evening at a banquet. Another messenger went to the home of Maximus Præclarus with a letter urging the young officer to attend an entertainment being given that same evening by a rich young patrician.

As both invitations had emanated from families high in favor with the Emperor, they were, in effect, almost equivalent to commands, even to as influential a senator as Dion Splendidus, and so there was no question either in the minds of the hosts or in the minds of the guests but that they would be accepted.

Night had fallen upon Castra Sanguinarius. Dion Splendidus and his wife were alighting from their litter before the home of their host and Maximus Præclarus was already drinking with his fellow guests in the banquet hall of one of Castra Sanguinarius's wealthiest citizens. Fastus was there, too, and Maximus Præclarus was surprised and not a little puzzled at the friendly attitude of the prince.

"I always suspect something when Fastus smiles at me," he said to an intimate.

In the home of Dion Splendidus, Dilecta sat among her female slaves, while one of them told her stories of the wild African village from which she had come.

Tarzan and Festivitas sat in the home of Maximus Præclarus, the Roman matron listening attentively to the stories of savage Africa and civilized Europe that she was constantly urging her strange guest to tell her. Faintly they heard a knock at the outer gate and, presently, a slave came to the apartment where they sat to tell them that Mpingu, the slave of Dion Splendidus, had come with a message for Tarzan.

"Bring him hither," said Festivitas, and, shortly, Mpingu was ushered into the room.

If Tarzan or Festivitas had known Mpingu better, they would have realized that he was under great nervous strain; but they did not know him well, and so they saw nothing out of the way in his manner or bearing.

"I have been sent to fetch you to the home of Dion Splendidus," said Mpingu to Tarzan.

"That is strange," said Festivitas.

"Your noble son stopped at the home of Dion Splendidus on his way to the banquet this evening and as he left I was summoned and told to come hither and fetch the stranger to my master's house," explained Mpingu. "That is all I know about the matter."

"Maximus Præclarus gave you those instructions himself?" asked Festivitas.

"Yes," replied Mpingu.

"I do not know what his reason can be," said Festivitas to Tarzan, "but there must be some very good reason, or he would not run the risk of your being caught."

"It is very dark out," said Mpingu. "No one will see him."

"There is no danger," said Tarzan to Festivitas. "Maximus Præclarus would not have sent for me unless it were necessary. Come, Mpingu!" And he arose, bidding Festivitas good-by.

Tarzan and Mpingu had proceeded but a short distance

down the avenue when the black motioned the ape-man to the side of the street, where a small gate was let into a solid wall.

"We are here," said Mpingu.

"This is not the home of Dion Splendidus," said Tarzan, immediately suspicious.

Mpingu was surprised that this stranger should so well remember the location of a house that he had visited but once, and that more than three weeks since, but he did not know the training that had been the ape-man's through the long years of moving through the trackless jungle that had trained his every sense and faculty to the finest point of orientation.

"It is not the main gate," replied Mpingu, quickly, "but Maximus Præclarus did not think it safe that you be seen entering the main gate of the home of Dion Splendidus in the event that, by any chance, you were observed. This way leads into a lane that might connect with any one of several homes, and once in it there is little or no chance of apprehension."

"I see," said Tarzan. "Lead the way."

Mpingu opened the gate and motioned Tarzan in ahead of him, and as the ape-man passed through into the blackness beyond there fell upon him what seemed to be a score of men and he was borne down in the same instant that he realized that he had been betrayed. So rapidly did his assailants work that it was a matter of seconds only before the ape-man found shackles upon his wrists, the one thing that he feared and hated most.

13

WHILE Erich von Harben wooed Favonia beneath a summer moon in the garden of Septimus Favonius in the island city of Castrum Mare, a detachment of the brown legionaries of Sublatus Imperator dragged Tarzan of the Apes and Mpingu, the slave of Dion Splendidus, to the dungeons beneath the Colosseum of Castra Sanguinarius—and far to the south a little monkey shivered from cold and terror in the topmost branches of a jungle giant, while Sheeta the panther crept softly through the black shadows far below.

In the banquet hall of his host, Maximus Præclarus reclined upon a sofa far down the board from Fastus, the guest of honor. The prince, his tongue loosed by frequent drafts of native wine, seemed in unusually good spirits, radiating self-satisfaction. Several times he had brought the subject of conversation around to the strange white barbarian, who had insulted his sire and twice escaped from the soldiers of Sublatus.

"He would never have escaped from me that day," he boasted, throwing a sneer in the direction of Maximus Præclarus, "nor from any other officer who is loyal to Cæsar."

"You had him, Fastus, in the garden of Dion Splendidus," retorted Præclarus. "Why did you not hold him?"

Fastus flushed. "I shall hold him this time," he blurted.

"This time?" queried Præclarus. "He has been captured again?" There was nothing in either the voice or expression of the young patrician of more than polite interest, though the words of Fastus had come with all the unexpected suddenness of lightning out of a clear sky.

"I mean," explained Fastus, in some confusion, "that if he is again captured I, personally, shall see that he does not escape," but his words did not allay the apprehensions of Præclarus.

All through the long dinner Præclarus was cognizant of a sensation of foreboding. There was a menace in the air that was apparent in the veiled hostility of his host and several others who were cronies of Fastus.

As early as was seemly he made his excuses and departed. Armed slaves accompanied his litter through the dark avenues of Castra Sanguinarius, where robbery and murder slunk among the shadows hand in hand with the criminal element that had been permitted to propagate itself without restraint; and when at last he came to the doorway at his home and had alighted from his litter he paused and a frown of perplexity clouded his face as he saw that the door stood partially ajar, though there was no slave there to receive him.

The house seemed unusually quiet and lifeless. The night light, which ordinarily a slave kept burning in the forecourt when a member of the household was away, was absent. For an instant Præclarus hesitated upon the threshold and then, throwing his cloak back from his shoulders to free his arms, he pushed the door open and stepped within.

In the banquet hall of a high court functionary the guests

yawned behind their hands from boredom, but none dared leave while Cæsar remained, for the Emperor was a guest there that evening. It was late when an officer brought a message to Sublatus—a message that the Emperor read with a satisfaction he made no effort to conceal.

"I have received an important message," said Sublatus to his host, "upon a matter that interests the noble Senator Dion Splendidus and his wife. It is my wish that you withdraw with the other guests, leaving us three here alone."

When they had gone he turned to Dion Splendidus. "It has long been rumored, Splendidus," he remarked, "that you aspire to the purple."

"A false rumor, Sublatus, as you should well know," replied the senator.

"I have reason to believe otherwise," said Sublatus, shortly. "There cannot be two Cæsars, Splendidus, and you well know the penalty for treason."

"If the Emperor has determined, for personal reasons or for any reason whatever, to destroy me, argument will avail me nothing," said Spendidus, haughtily.

"But I have other plans," said Sublatus, "—plans that might be overturned should I cause your death."

"Yes?" inquired Splendidus, politely.

"Yes," assented Sublatus. "My son wishes to marry your daughter, Dilecta, and it is also my wish, for thus would the two most powerful families of Castra Sanguinarius be united and the future of the empire assured."

"But our daughter, Dilecta, is betrothed to another," said Splendidus.

"To Maximus Præclarus?" inquired Sublatus.

"Yes," replied the senator.

"Then let me tell you that she shall never wed Maximus Præclarus," said the Emperor.

"Why?" inquired Splendidus.

"Because Maximus Præclarus is about to die."

"I do not understand," said Splendidus.

"Perhaps when I tell you that the white barbarian, Tarzan, has been captured, you will understand why Præclarus is about to die," said Sublatus, with a sneer.

Dion Splendidus shook his head negatively. "I regret," he said, "that I do not follow Cæsar."

"I think you do, Splendidus," said the Emperor, "but that is neither here nor there, since it is Cæsar's will that there be no breath of suspicion upon the sire of the next Empress of Castra Sanguinarius. So permit me to explain what I am sure that you already know. After the white barbarian escaped from my soldiers he was found by Maximus Præclarus in your garden. My son, Fastus, witnessed the capture. One of your own slaves acted as interpreter between the barbarian and Maximus, who arranged that the barbarian should escape and take refuge in the home of Maximus. Tonight he was found there and captured, and Maximus Præclarus has been placed under arrest. They are both in the dungeons beneath the Colosseum. It is improbable that these things should have transpired entirely without your knowledge, but I shall let it pass if you give your word that Dilecta shall marry Fastus."

"During the entire history of Castra Sanguinarius," said Dion Splendidus, "it has been our boast that our daughters have been free to choose their own husbands—not even a Cæsar might command a free woman to marry against her will."

"That is true," replied Sublatus, "and for that very reason I do not command—I am only advising."

"I cannot answer for my daughter," said Splendidus. "Let the son of Cæsar do his own wooing as becomes the men of Castra Sanguinarius."

Sublatus arose. "I am only advising," but his tone belied his words. "The noble senator and his wife may retire to their home and give thought to what Cæsar has said. In the course of a few days Fastus will come for his answer."

By the light of the torch that illuminated the interior of the dungeon into which he was thrust by his captors, Tarzan saw a white man and several Negroes chained to the walls. Among the blacks was Lukedi, but when he recognized Tarzan he evinced only the faintest sign of interest, so greatly had his confinement weighed upon his mind and altered him.

The ape-man was chained next to the only other white in the dungeon, and he could not help but notice the keen interest that this prisoner took in him from the moment that he entered until the soldiers withdrew, taking the torch with them, leaving the dungeon in darkness.

As had been his custom while he was in the home of Maximus Præclarus, Tarzan had worn only his loincloth and leopard skin, with a toga and sandals out of courtesy for Festivitas when he appeared in her presence. This evening, when he started out with Mpingu, he had worn the toga as a disguise, but in the scuffle that preceeded his capture it had been torn from him, with the result that his appearance was sufficient to arouse the curiosity of his fellow prisoners, and as soon as the guards were out of hearing the man spoke to him.

"Can it be," he asked, "that you are the white barbarian whose fame has penetrated even to the gloom and silence of the dungeon?"

"I am Tarzan of the Apes," replied the ape-man.

"And you carried Sublatus out of his palace above your head and mocked at his soldiers!" exclaimed the other. "By the ashes of my imperial father, Sublatus will see that you die the death."

Tarzan made no reply.

"They say you run through the trees like a monkey," said the other. "How then did you permit yourself to be recaptured?"

"It was done by treachery," replied Tarzan, "and the quickness with which they locked the shackles upon me. Without these," and he shook the manacles upon his wrists, "they could not hold me. But who are you and what did you do to get yourself in the dungeons of Cæsar?"

"I am in the dungeon of no Cæsar," replied the other. "This creature who sits upon the throne of Castra Sanguinarius is no Cæsar."

"Who then is Cæsar?" inquired Tarzan.

"Only the Emperors of the East are entitled to be called Cæsar," replied the other.

"I take it that you are not of Castra Sanguinarius then," suggested the ape-man.

"No," replied the other, "I am from Castrum Mare."

"And why are you a prisoner?" asked Tarzan.

"Because I am from Castrum Mare," replied the other.

"Is that a crime in Castra Sanguinarius?" asked the ape-man.

"We are always enemies," replied the other. "We trade occasionally under a flag of truce, for we have things that they want and they have things that we must have, but there is much raiding and often there are wars, and then whichever side is victorious takes the things by force that otherwise they would be compelled to pay for."

"In this small valley what is there that one of you may have that the other one has not already?" asked the ape-man.

"We of Castrum Mare have the iron mines," replied the other, "and we have the papyrus swamps and the lake, which give us many things that the people of Castra Sanguinarius can obtain only from us. We sell them iron and paper, ink, snails, fish, and jewels, and many manufactured articles. In their end of the valley they mine gold, and as they control the only entrance to the country from the outside world, we are forced to obtain our slaves through them as well as new breeding-stock for our herds.

"As the Sanguinarians are naturally thieves and raiders and are too lazy to work and too ignorant to teach their slaves how to produce things, they depend entirely upon their gold mine and their raiding and trading with the outer world, while we, who have developed many skilled artisans, have been in a position for many generations that permitted us to obtain much more gold and many more slaves than we need in return for our manufactured articles. Today we are much richer than the Sanguinarians. We live better. We are more cultured. We are happier and the Sanguinarians are jealous and their hatred of us has increased."

"Knowing these things," asked Tarzan, "how is it that you came to the country of your enemies and permitted yourself to be captured?"

"I was delivered over treacherously into the hands of Sublatus by my uncle, Validus Augustus, Emperor of the East," replied the other. "My name is Cassius Hasta, and my father was Emperor before Validus. Validus is afraid that I may wish to seize the purple, and for this reason he plotted to get rid of me without assuming any responsibility for the act; so he conceived the idea of sending me upon a military mission, after bribing one of the servants who accompanied me to deliver me into the hands of Sublatus."

"What will Sublatus do with you?" asked Tarzan.

"The same thing that he will do with you," replied Cassius Hasta. "We shall be exhibited in the triumph of Sublatus, which he holds annually, and then in the arena we shall amuse them until we are slain."

"And when does this take place?" asked Tarzan.

"It will not be long now," replied Cassius Hasta. "Already they have collected so many prisoners to exhibit in the triumph and to take part in the combats in the arena that they are forced to confine Negroes and whites in the same dungeons, a thing they do not ordinarily do."

"Are these Negroes held here for this purpose?" asked the ape-man.

"Yes," replied the other.

Tarzan turned in the direction of Lukedi, whom he could not see in the darkness. "Lukedi!" he called.

"What is it?" asked the black, listlessly.

"You are well?" asked Tarzan.

"I am going to die," replied Lukedi. "They will feed me to lions or burn me upon a cross or make me fight with other warriors, so that it will be all the same for Lukedi. It was a sad day when Nyuto, the chief, captured Tarzan."

"Are all these men from your village?" asked Tarzan.

"No," replied Lukedi. "Most of them are from the villages outside the walls of Castra Sanguinarius."

"Yesterday they called us their own people," spoke up a man, who understood the language of the Bagego, "and tomorrow they make us kill one another to entertain Cæsar."

95

"You must be very few in numbers or very poor in spirit," said Tarzan, "that you submit to such treatment."

"We number nearly twice as many as the people in the city," said the man, "and we are brave warriors."

"Then you are fools," said Tarzan.

"We shall not be fools forever. Already there are many who would rise against Sublatus and the whites of Castra Sanguinarius."

"The Negroes of the city as well as those of the outer villages hate Cæsar," said Mpingu, who had been brought to the dungeon with Tarzan.

The statements of the men furnished food for thought to Tarzan. He knew that in the city there must be hundreds and perhaps thousands of African slaves and many thousands of others in the outer villages. If a leader should arise among them, the tyranny of Cæsar might be brought to an abrupt end. He spoke of the matter to Cassius Hasta, but the patrician assured him that no such leader would ever arise.

"We have dominated them for so many centuries," he explained, "that fear of us is an inherited instinct. Our slaves will never rise against their masters."

"But if they did?" asked Tarzan.

"Unless they had a white leader they could not succeed," replied Hasta.

"And why not a white leader then?" asked Tarzan.

"That is unthinkable," replied Hasta.

Their conversation was interrupted by the arrival of a detachment of soldiers, and as they halted before the entrance to the dungeon and threw open the gate Tarzan saw, in the light of their torches, that they were bringing another prisoner. As they dragged the man in, he recognized Maximus Præclarus. He saw that Præclarus recognized him, but as the Roman did not address him, Tarzan kept silent, too. The soldiers chained Præclarus to the wall, and after they had left and the dungeon was in darkness again, the young officer spoke.

"I see now why I am here," said Præclarus, "but even when they set upon me and arrested me in the vestibule of my home, I had guessed as much, after piecing together the insinuations of Fastus at the banquet this evening."

"I have been fearful that by befriending me you would bring disaster upon yourself," said Tarzan.

"Do not reproach yourself," said Præclarus. "Fastus or Sublatus would have found another excuse. I have been doomed from the moment that the attention of Fastus fixed itself upon Dilecta. To attain his end it was necessary that

I be destroyed. That is all, my friend, but yet I wonder who it could have been that betrayed me."

"It was I," said a voice out of the darkness.

"Who is that that speaks?" demanded Præclarus.

"It is Mpingu," said Tarzan. "He was arrested with me when we were on the way to the home of Dion Splendidus to meet you."

"To meet me!" exclaimed Præclarus.

"I lied," said Mpingu, "but they made me."

"Who made you?" demanded Præclarus.

"The officers of Cæsar and Cæsar's son," replied Mpingu. "They dragged me to the palace of the Emperor and held me down upon my back and brought tongs to tear out my tongue and hot irons to burn out my eyes. Oh, master, what else could I do? I am only a poor slave and I was afraid and Cæsar is very terrible."

"I understand," said Præclarus. "I do not blame you, Mpingu."

"They promised to give me my liberty," said the slave, "but instead they have chained me in this dungeon. Doubtless I shall die in the arena, but that I do not fear. It was the tongs and the red-hot irons that made me a coward. Nothing else could have forced me to betray the friend of my master."

There was little comfort upon the cold, hard stones of the dungeon floor, but Tarzan, inured to hardship from birth, slept soundly until the coming of the jailer with food awakened him several hours after sunrise. Water and coarse bread were doled out to the inmates of the dungeon by slaves in charge of a surly half-caste in the uniform of a legionary.

As he ate, Tarzan surveyed his fellow prisoners. There was Cassius Hasta of Castrum Mare, son of a Cæsar, and Maximus Præclarus, a patrician of Castra Sanguinarius and captain of Legionaries. These, with himself, were the only whites. There was Lukedi, the Bagego who had befriended him in the village of Nyuto, and Mpingu, the slave of Dion Splendidus, who had betrayed him, and now, in the light from the little barred window, he recognized also another Bagego—Ogonyo, who still cast fearful eyes upon Tarzan as one might upon any person who was on familiar terms with the ghost of one's grandfather.

In addition to these three, there were five strapping warriors from the outer villages of Castra Sanguinarius, picked men chosen because of their superb physiques for the gladiatorial contests that would form so important a part of the games that would shortly take place in the arena for the glorification of Cæsar and the edification of the masses. The small room was so crowded that there was barely space upon the floor for the eleven to stretch their bodies, yet there was one vacant ring in the stone wall, indicating that the full capacity of the dungeon had not been reached.

Two days and nights dragged slowly by. The inmates of the cell amused themselves as best they could, though the Negroes were too downcast to take a lively interest in anything other than their own sad forebodings.

Tarzan talked much with these and especially with the five warriors from the outer villages. From long experience with them he knew the minds and the hearts of these men, and it was not difficult for him to win their confidence and, presently, he was able to instil within them something of his own courageous self-reliance, which could never accept or admit absolute defeat.

He talked with Præclarus about Castra Sanguinarius and with Cassius Hasta about Castrum Mare. He learned all that they could tell him about the forthcoming triumph and games; about the military methods of their people, their laws and their customs until he, who all his life had been accounted taciturn, might easily have been indicted for loquacity by his fellow prisoners, yet, though they might not realize it, he asked them nothing without a well-defined purpose.

Upon the third day of his incarceration another prisoner was brought to the crowded cell in which Tarzan was chained. He was a young white man in the tunic and cuirass of an officer. He was received in silence by the other prisoners, as seemed to be the custom among them, but after he had been fastened to the remaining ring and the soldiers who had brought him had departed, Cassius Hasta greeted him with suppressed excitement.

"Cæcilius Metellus!" he exclaimed.

The other turned in the direction of Hasta's voice, his eyes not yet accustomed to the gloom of the dungeon.

"Hasta!" he exclaimed. "I would know that voice were I to hear it rising from the blackest depths of Tartarus."

"What ill fortune brought you here?" demanded Hasta.

"It is no ill fortune that unites me with my best friend," replied Metellus.

"But tell me how it happened," insisted Cassius Hasta.

"Many things have happened since you left Castrum Mare," replied Metellus. "Fulvus Fupus has wormed his way into the favor of the Emperor to such an extent that all of your former friends are under suspicion and in actual danger. Mallius Lepus is in prison. Septimus Favonius is out of favor with the Emperor and would be in prison himself were it not that Fupus is in love with Favonia, his daughter. But the most outrageous news that I have to communicate to you is that

Validus Augustus has adopted Fulvus Fupus and has named him as his successor to the imperial purple."

"Fupus a Cæsar!" cried Hasta, in derision. "And sweet Favonia? It cannot be that she favors Fulvus Fupus?"

"No," replied Metellus, "and that fact lies at the bottom of all the trouble. She loves another, and Fupus, in his desire to possess her, has utilized the Emperor's jealousy of you to destroy every obstacle that stands in his way."

"And whom does Favonia love?" asked Cassius Hasta. "It cannot be Mallius Lepus, her cousin?"

"No," replied Metellus, "it is a stranger. One whom you have never known."

"How can that be?" demanded Cassius Hasta. "Do I not know every patrician in Castrum Mare?"

"He is not of Castrum Mare."

"Not a Sanguinarian?" demanded Cassius Hasta.

"No, he is a barbarian chieftain from Germania."

"What nonsense is this?" demanded Hasta.

"I speak the truth," replied Metellus. "He came shortly after you departed from Castrum Mare, and being a scholar well versed in the history of ancient and modern Rome he won the favor of Validus Augustus, but he brought ruin upon himself and upon Mallius Lepus and upon Septimus Favonius by winning the love of Favonia and with it the jealous hatred of Fulvus Fupus."

"What is his name?" asked Cassius Hasta.

"He calls himself Erich von Harben," replied Metellus.

"Erich von Harben," repeated Tarzan. "I know him. Where is he now? Is he safe?"

Cæcilius Metellus turned his eyes in the direction of the ape-man. "How do you know Erich von Harben, Sanguinarian?" he demanded. "Perhaps then the story that Fulvus Fupus told Validus Augustus is true—that this Erich von Harben is in reality a spy from Castra Sanguinarius."

"No," said Maximus Præclarus. "Do not excite yourself. This Erich von Harben has never been in Castra Sanguinarius, and my friend here is not himself a Sanguinarian. He is a white barbarian from the outer world, and if his story be true, and I have no reason to doubt it, he came here in search of this Erich von Harben."

"You may believe this story, Metellus," said Cassius Hasta. "These both are honorable men and since we have been in prison together we have become good friends. What they tell you is the truth."

"Tell me something of von Harben," insisted Tarzen. "Where is he now and is he in danger from the machinations of this Fulvus Fupus?"

"He is in prison with Mallius Lepus in Castrum Mare,"

replied Metellus, "and if he survives the games, which he will not, Fupus will find some other means to destroy him."

"When are the games held?" asked Tarzan.

"They start upon the ides of August," replied Cassius Hasta.

"And it is now about the nones of August," said Tarzan.

"Tomorrow," corrected Praeclarus.

"We shall know it then," said Cassius Hasta, "for that is the date set for the triumph of Sublatus."

"I am told that the games last about a week," said Tarzan. "How far is it to Castrum Mare?"

"Perhaps an eight hours' march for fresh troops," said Caecilius Metellus; "but why do you ask? Are you planning on making a trip to Castrum Mare?"

Tarzan noted the other's smile and the ironic tone of his voice. "I am going to Castrum Mare," he said.

"Perhaps you will take us with you," laughed Metellus.

"Are you a friend of von Harben?" asked Tarzan.

"I am a friend of his friends and an enemy of his enemies, but I do not know him well enough to say that he is my friend."

"But you have no love for Validus Augustus, the Emperor?" asked Tarzan.

"No," replied the other.

"And I take it that Cassius Hasta has no reason to love his uncle, either?" continued Tarzan.

"You are right," said Hasta.

"Perhaps I shall take you both, then," said Tarzan.

The two men laughed.

"We shall be ready to go with you when you are ready to take us," said Cassius Hasta.

"You may count me in on the party, too," said Maximus Praeclarus, "if Cassius Hasta will remain my friend in Castrum Mare."

"That I promise, Maximus Praeclarus," said Cassius Hasta.

"When do we leave?" demanded Metellus, shaking his chain.

"I can leave the moment that these shackles are struck from me," said the ape-man, "and that they must do when they turn me into the arena to fight."

"There will be many legionaries to see that you do not escape, you may rest assured of that," Cassius Hasta reminded him.

"Maximus Praeclarus will tell you that I have twice escaped from the legionaries of Sublatus," said Tarzan.

"That he has," declared Praeclarus. "Surrounded by the Emperor's guard, he escaped from the very throne-room of Sublatus and he carried Caesar above his head through the length of the palace and out into the avenue beyond."

"But if I am to take you with me, it will be more difficult," said the ape-man, "and I would take you because it would please me to frustrate the plans of Sublatus and also because two of you, at least, could be helpful to me in finding Erich von Harben in the city of Castrum Mare."

"You interest me," said Cassius Hasta. "You almost make me believe that you can accomplish this mad scheme."

14

A GREAT sun, rising into a cloudless sky, ushered in the nones of August. It looked down upon the fresh-raked sands of the deserted arena; upon the crowds that lined the Via Principalis that bisected Castra Sanguinarius.

Brown artisans and tradesmen in their smart tunics jostled one another for places of vantage along the shady avenue. Among them moved barbarians from the outer villages, sporting their finest feathers and most valued ornaments and skins, and mingling with the others were the slaves of the city, all eagerly waiting for the pageant that would inaugurate the triumph of Sublatus.

Upon the low rooftops of their homes the patricians reclined upon rugs at every point where the avenue might be seen between or beneath the branches of the trees. All Castra Sanguinarius was there, technically to honor Cæsar, but actually merely to be entertained.

The air buzzed with talk and laughter; hawkers of sweetmeats and trinkets elbowed through the crowd crying their wares; legionaries posted at intervals the full distance from the palace to the Colosseum kept the center of the avenue clear.

Since the evening of the preceding day the throng had been gathering. During the cold night they had huddled with close-drawn cloaks. There had been talk and laughter and brawls and near-riots, and many would-be spectators had been haled off to the dungeons where their exuberance might be permitted to cool against cold stone.

As the morning dragged on the crowd became restless. At first, as some patrician who was to have a part in the pageant passed in his ornate litter he would be viewed in respectful and interested silence, or if he were well known and favorably thought of by the multitude he might be greeted with cheers; but with the passing of time and the increasing heat of the day each occasional litter that passed elicited deep-throated groans or raucous catcalls as the patience and the temper of the mob became thinner.

But presently from afar, in the direction of the palace, sounded the martial notes of trumpets. The people forgot their fatigue and their discomfort as the shrill notes galvanized them into joyous expectancy.

Slowly along the avenue came the pageant, led by a score of trumpeters, behind whom marched a maniple of the imperial guard. Waving crests surmounted their burnished helmets, the metal of two hundred cuirasses, pikes, and shields shot back the sunlight that filtered through the trees beneath which they marched. They made a proud showing as they strode haughtily between the lines of admiring eyes, led by their patrician officers in gold and embossed leather and embroidered linen.

As the legionaries passed, a great shout of applause arose. A roar of human voices that started at the palace rolled slowly along the Via Principalis toward the Colosseum as Cæsar himself, resplendent in purple and gold, rode alone in a chariot drawn by lions led on golden leashes by huge blacks.

Cæsar may have expected for himself the plaudits of the populace, but there was a question as to whether these were elicited as much by the presence of the Emperor as by the sight of the captives chained to Cæsar's chariot, for Cæsar was an old story to the people of Castra Sanguinarius, while the prisoners were a novelty and, furthermore, something that promised rare sport in the arena.

Never before in the memory of the citizens of Castra Sanguinarius had an Emperor exhibited such noteworthy captives in his triumph. There was Nyuto, the chief of the Bagegos. There was Cæcilius Metellus, a centurion of the legions of the Emperor of the East; and Cassius Hasta, the nephew of that Emperor; but perhaps he who aroused their greatest enthusiasm because of the mad stories that had been narrated of his feats of strength and agility was the great white barbarian, with a shock of black hair and his well-worn leopard skin.

The collar of gold and the golden chain that held him in leash to the chariot of Cæsar, curiously enough, imparted to his appearance no suggestion of fear or humiliation. He walked proudly with head erect—a lion tethered to lions—and there was that in the easy sinuosity of his stride that accentuated his likeness to the jungle beasts that drew the chariot of Cæsar along the broad Via Principalis of Castra Sanguinarius.

As the pageant moved its length slowly to the Colosseum the crowd found other things to hold their interest. There were the Bagego captives chained neck to neck and stalwart gladiators resplendent in new armor. White men and brown men were numbered among these and many warriors from the outer villages.

To the number of two hundred they marched—captives, condemned criminals, and professional gladiators—but before them and behind them and on either side marched veteran legionaries whose presence spoke in no uncertain terms of the respect in which Cæsar held the potential power of these bitter, savage fighting-men.

There were floats depicting historic events in the history of Castra Sanguinarius and ancient Rome. There were litters bearing the high officers of the court and the senators of the city, while bringing up the rear were the captured flocks and herds of the Bagegos.

That Sublatus failed to exhibit Maximus Præclarus in his triumph evidenced the popularity of this noble young Roman, but Dilecta, watching the procession from the roof of her father's house, was filled with anxiety when she noted the absence of her lover, for she knew that sometimes men who entered the dungeons of Cæsar were never heard of more—but there was none who could tell her whether Maximus Præclarus lived or not, and so with her mother she made her way to the Colosseum to witness the opening of the games. Her heart was heavy lest she should see Maximus Præclarus entered there, and his blood upon the white sand, yet, also, she feared that she might not see him and thus be faced by the almost definite assurance that he had been secretly done to death by the agents of Fastus.

A great multitude had gathered in the Colosseum to witness the entry of Cæsar and the pageant of his triumph, and the majority of these remained in their seats for the opening of the games, which commenced early in the afternoon. It was not until then that the sections reserved for the patricians began to fill.

The loge reserved for Dion Splendidus, the senator, was close to that of Cæsar. It afforded an excellent view of the arena and with cushions and rugs was so furnished as to afford the maximum comfort to those who occupied it.

Never had a Cæsar essayed so pretentious a fête; entertainment of the rarest description was vouchsafed each lucky spectator, yet never before in her life had Dilecta loathed and dreaded any occurrence as she now loathed and dreaded the games that were about to open.

Always heretofore her interest in the contestants had been impersonal. Professional gladiators were not of the class to come within the ken or acquaintance of the daughter of a patrician. The warriors and slaves were to her of no greater importance than the beasts against which they sometimes contended, while the condemned criminals, many of whom expiated their sins within the arena, aroused within her heart only the remotest suggestion of sympathy. She was a sweet and lovely girl, whose sensibilities would doubtless have been shocked by the brutality of the prize-ring or a varsity football game, but she could look upon the bloody cruelties of a Roman arena without a qualm, because by custom and heredity they had become a part of the national life of her people.

But today she trembled. She saw the games as a personal menace to her own happiness and the life of one she loved, yet by no outward sign did she divulge her perturbation. Calm, serene, and entirely beautiful, Dilecta, the daughter of Dion Splendidus, awaited the signal for the opening of the games that was marked by the arrival of Cæsar.

Sublatus came, and after he had taken his seat there emerged from one of the barred gates at the far end of the arena the head of a procession, again led by trumpeters, who were followed by those who were to take part in the games during the week. It consisted for the most part of the same captives who had been exhibited in the pageant, to which were added a number of wild beasts, some of which were led or dragged along by slaves, while others, more powerful and ferocious, were drawn in wheeled cages. These consisted principally of lions and leopards, but there were also a couple of bull buffaloes and several cages in which were confined huge man-like apes.

The participants were formed in a solid phalanx facing Sublatus, where they were addressed by the Emperor, freedom and reward being promised the victors; and then, sullen and lowering, they were herded back to their dungeons and cages.

Dilecta's eyes scanned the faces of the contestants as they stood in solid rank before the loge of Cæsar, but nowhere among them could she discover Maximus Præclarus. Breathless and tense, with fearful apprehension, she leaned forward in her seat across the top of the arena wall as a man entered the loge from behind and sat upon the bench beside her.

"He is not there," said the man.

The girl turned quickly toward the speaker. "Fastus!" she exclaimed. "How do you know that he is not there?"

"It is by my order," replied the prince.

"He is dead," cried Dilecta. "You have had him killed."

"No," denied Fastus, "he is safe in his cell."

"What is to become of him?" asked the girl.

"His fate lies in your hands," replied Fastus. "Give him up and promise to become the wife of Fastus and I will see that he is not forced to appear in the arena."

"He would not have it so," said the girl.

Fastus shrugged. "As you will," he said, "but remember that his life is in your hands."

"With sword, or dagger, or pike he has no equal," said the girl, proudly. "If he were entered in the contest, he would be victorious."

"Cæsar has been known to pit unarmed men against lions," Fastus reminded her, tauntingly. "Of what avail then is prowess with any weapon?"

"That would be murder," said Dilecta.

"A harsh term to apply to an act of Cæsar," returned Fastus, menacingly.

"I speak my mind," said the girl; "Cæsar or no Cæsar. It would be a cowardly and contemptible act, but I doubt not that either Cæsar or his son is capable of even worse." Her voice trembled with scathing contempt.

With a crooked smile upon his lips, Fastus arose. "It is not a matter to be determined without thought," he said, "and your answer concerns not Maximus Præclarus alone, nor you, nor me."

"What do you mean?" she asked.

"There are Dion Splendidus and your mother, and Festivitas, the mother of Præclarus!" And with this warning he turned and left the loge.

The games progressed amid the din of trumpets, the crash of arms, the growling of beasts, and the murmuring of the great audience that sometimes rose to wild acclaim or deep-throated, menacing disapproval. Beneath fluttering banners and waving scarfs the cruel, terrible thousand-eyed thing that is a crowd looked down upon the blood and suffering of its fellow men, munching sweetmeats while a victim died and cracking coarse jokes as slaves dragged the body from the arena and raked clean sand over crimsoned spots.

Sublatus had worked long and carefully with the præfect in charge of the games that the resultant program might afford the greatest possible entertainment for Cæsar and the populace, thus winning for the Emperor a certain popularity that his own personality did not command.

Always the most popular events were those in which men of the patrician class participated, and so he counted much upon Cassius Hasta and Cæcilius Metellus, but of even greater value for his purpose was the giant white barbarian, who already had captured the imagination of the people because of his exploits.

Wishing to utilize Tarzan in as many events as possible, Sublatus knew that it would be necessary to reserve the more dangerous ones for the latter part of the week, and so upon the first afternoon of the games Tarzan found himself thrust into the arena, unarmed, in company with a burly murderer, whom the master of the games had clothed in loincloth and leopard skin similar to Tarzan.

A guard escorted them across the arena and halted them in the sand below the Emperor, where the master of the games announced that these two would fight with bare hands in any way that they saw fit and that he who remained alive or alone in the arena at the end of the combat would be considered victorious.

"The gate to the dungeons will be left open," he said, "and if either contestant gets enough he may quit the arena, but whoever does so forfeits the contest to the other."

The crowd booed. It was not to see such tame exhibitions as this that they had come to the Colosseum. They wanted blood. They wanted thrills, but they waited, for perhaps this contest might afford comedy—that they enjoyed, too. If one greatly outclassed the other, it would be amusing to see the weaker seek escape. They cheered Tarzan and they cheered the low-browed murderer. They shouted insults at the noble patrician who was master of the games, for they knew the safety and irresponsibility of numbers.

As the word was given the contestants to engage one another Tarzan turned to face the low-browed, hulking brute against whom he had been pitted and he saw that some one had been at pains to select a worthy antagonist for him. The man was somewhat shorter than Tarzan, but great, hard muscles bulged beneath his brown hide, bulking so thick across his back and shoulders as almost to suggest deformity. His long arms hung almost to his knees, and his thick, gnarled legs suggested a man of bronze upon a pedestal of granite. The fellow circled Tarzan, looking for an opening. He scowled ferociously as though to frighten his adversary.

"There is the gate, barbarian," he cried in a low voice, pointing to the far end of the arena. "Escape while you are yet alive."

The crowd roared in approbation. It enjoyed glorious sallies such as these. "I shall tear you limb from limb," shouted the murderer, and again the crowd applauded.

"I am here," said Tarzan, calmly.

"Flee!" screamed the murderer, and lowering his head he charged like an angry bull.

The ape-man sprang into the air and came down upon

106

his antagonist, and what happened happened so quickly that no one there, other than Tarzan, knew how it had been accomplished; only he knew that he clamped a reverse headlock upon the murderer.

What the crowd saw was the hulking figure hurtling to a hard fall. They saw him lying half-stunned upon the sand, while the giant barbarian stood with folded arms looking down upon him.

The fickle crowd rose from its benches, shrieking with delight. *"Habet! Habet!"* they cried, and thousands of closed fists were outstretched with the thumbs pointing downward, but Tarzan only stood there waiting, as the murderer, shaking his head to clear his brain, crawled slowly to his feet.

The fellow looked about him half-bewildered and then his eyes found Tarzan and with a growl of rage he charged again. Again the terrible hold was clamped upon him, and again he was hurled heavily to the floor of the arena.

The crowd screamed with delight. Every thumb in the Colosseum was pointed downward. They wanted Tarzan to kill his adversary. The ape-man looked up into Cæsar's loge, where sat the master of the games with Sublatus.

"Is not this enough?" he demanded, pointing at the prostrate figure of the stunned gladiator.

The præfect waved a hand in an all-including gesture which took in the audience. "They demand his death," he said. "While he remains alive in the arena, you are not the victor."

"Does Cæsar require that I kill this defenseless man?" demanded Tarzan, looking straight into the face of Sublatus.

"You have heard the noble præfect," replied the Emperor, haughtily.

"Good," said Tarzan. "The rules of the contest shall be fulfilled." He stooped and seized the unconscious form of his antagonist and raised it above his head. "Thus I carried your Emperor from his throne-room to the avenue!" he shouted to the audience.

Screams of delight measured the appreciation of the populace, while Cæsar went white and red in anger and mortification. He half rose from his seat, but what he contemplated was never fulfilled, for at that instant Tarzen swung the body of the murderer downward and back like a huge pendulum and then upward with a mighty surge, hurling it over the arena wall, full into the loge of Sublatus, where it struck Cæsar, knocking him to the floor.

"I am alive and alone in the arena," shouted Tarzan, turning to the people, "and by the terms of the contest I am victor," and not even Cæsar dared question the decision that was voiced by the shrieking, screaming, applauding multitude.

15

B LOODY days followed restless nights in comfortless cells,
where lice and rats joined forces to banish rest. When
the games began there had been twelve inmates in the
cell occupied by Tarzan, but now three empty rings dangled
against the stone wall, and each day they wondered whose
turn was next.

The others did not reproach Tarzan because of his failure
to free them, since they had never taken his optimism se-
riously. They could not conceive of contestants escaping from
the arena during the games. It simply was not done and that
was all that there was to it. It never had been done, and
it never would be.

"We know you meant well," said Præclarus, "but we knew
better than you."

"The conditions have not been right, as yet," said Tarzan,
"but if what I have been told of the games is true, the time
will come."

"What time could be propitious," asked Hasta, "while more
than half of Cæsar's legionaries packed the Colosseum?"

"There should be a time," Tarzan reminded him, "when all
the victorious contestants are in the arena together. Then we
shall rush Cæsar's loge and drag him into the arena. With
Sublatus as a hostage we may demand a hearing and get it.
I venture to say that they will give us our liberty in return
for Cæsar."

"But how can we enter Cæsar's loge?" demanded Metellus.

"In an instant we may form steps with living men stoop-
ing, while others step upon their backs as soldiers scale a
wall. Perhaps some of us will be killed, but enough will succeed to seize Cæsar and drag him to the sands."

"I wish you luck," said Præclarus, "and, by Jupiter, I believe that you will succeed. I only wish that I might be with
you."

"You will not accompany us?" demanded Tarzan.

"How can I? I shall be locked in this cell. Is it not evident that they do not intend to enter me in the contests?
They are reserving for me some other fate. The jailer has told
me that my name appears in no event."

"But we must find a way to take you with us," said Tarzan.

"There is no way," said Præclarus, shaking his head, sadly.

"Wait," said Tarzan. "You commanded the Colosseum guards, did you not?"

"Yes," replied Præclarus.

"And you had the keys to the cells?" asked the ape-man.

"Yes," replied Præclarus, "and to the manacles as well."

"Where are they?" asked Tarzan. "But no, that will not do. They must have taken them from you when they arrested you."

"No, they did not," said Præclarus. "As a matter of fact, I did not have them with me when I dressed for the banquet that night. I left them in my room."

"But perhaps they sent for them?"

"Yes, they sent for them, but they did not find them. The jailer asked me about them the day after I was arrested, but I told him that the soldiers took them from me. I told him that because I had hidden them in a secret place where I keep many valuables. I knew that if I had told them where they were they would take not only the keys, but my valuables as well."

"Good!" exclaimed the ape-man. "With the keys our problem is solved."

"But how are you going to get them?" demanded Præclarus, with a rueful smile.

"I do not know," said Tarzan. "All I know is that we must have the keys."

"We know, too, that we should have our liberty," said Hasta, "but knowing it does not make us free."

Their conversation was interrupted by the approach of soldiers along the corridor. Presently a detachment of the palace guard halted outside their cell. The jailer unlocked the door and a man entered with two torch-bearers behind him. It was Fastus.

He looked around the cell. "Where is Præclarus?" he demanded, and then, "Ah, there you are!"

Præclarus did not reply.

"Stand up, slave!" ordered Fastus, arrogantly. "Stand up, all of you. How dare you sit in the presence of a Cæsar!" he exclaimed.

"Swine is a better title for such as you," taunted Præclarus.

"Drag them up! Beat them with your pikes!" cried Fastus to the soldiers outside the doorway.

The command of the Colosseum guard, who stood just behind Fastus, blocked the doorway. "Stand back," he said to the legionaries. "No one gives orders here except Cæsar and myself, and you are not Cæsar yet, Fastus."

"I shall be one day," snapped the prince, "and it will be a sad day for you."

"It will be a sad day for all Castra Sanguinarius," replied the officer. "You said that you wished to speak to Præclarus? Say what you have to say and be gone. Not even Cæsar's son may interfere with my charges."

Fastus trembled with anger, but he knew that he was powerless. The commander of the guard spoke with the authority of the Emperor, whom he represented. He turned upon Præclarus.

"I came to invite my good friend, Maximus Præclarus, to my wedding," he announced, with a sneer. He waited, but Præclarus made no reply. "You do not seem duly impressed, Præclarus," continued the prince. "You do not ask who is to be the happy bride. Do you not wish to know who will be the next Empress in Castra Sanguinarius, even though you may not live to see her upon the throne beside Cæsar?"

The heart of Maximus Præclarus stood still, for now he knew why Fastus had come to the dungeon-cell, but he gave no sign of what was passing within his breast, but remained seated in silence upon the hard floor, his back against the cold wall.

"You do not ask me whom I am to wed, nor when," continued Fastus, "but I shall tell you. You should be interested. Dilecta, the daughter of Dion Splendidus, will have none of a traitor and a felon. She aspires to share the purple with a Cæsar. In the evening following the last day of the games Dilecta and Fastus are to be married in the throne-room of the palace."

Gloating, Fastus waited to know the result of his announcement, but if he had looked to surprise Maximus Præclarus into an exhibition of chagrin he failed, for the young patrician ignored him so completely that Fastus might not have been in the cell at all for all the attention that the other paid to him.

Maximus Præclarus turned and spoke casually to Metellus and the quiet affront aroused the mounting anger of Fastus to such an extent that he lost what little control he had of himself. Stepping quickly forward, he stooped and slapped Præclarus in the face and then spat upon him, but in doing so he had come too close to Tarzan and the ape-man reached out and seized him by the ankle, dragging him to the floor.

Fastus screamed a command to his soldiers. He sought to draw his dagger or his sword, but Tarzan took them from him and hurled the prince into the arms of the legionaries, who had rushed past the commander of the Colosseum guard and entered the cell.

"Get out now, Fastus," said the latter. "You have caused enough trouble here already."

"I shall get you for this," hissed the prince, "all of you," and he swept the inmates of the cell with an angry, menacing glance.

Long after they had gone, Cassius Hasta continued to chuckle. "Cæsar!" he exclaimed. "Swine!"

As the prisoners discussed the discomfiture of Fastus and sought to prophesy what might come of it, they saw a wavering light reflected from afar in the corridor before their cell.

"We are to have more guests," said Metellus.

"Perhaps Fastus is returning to spit on Tarzan," suggested Cassius Hasta, and they all laughed.

The light was advancing along the corridor, but it was not accompanied by the tramp of soldiers' feet.

"Whoever comes comes silently and alone," said Maximus Præclarus.

"Then it is not Fastus," said Hasta.

"But it might be an assassin sent by him," suggested Præclarus.

"We shall be ready for him," said Tarzan.

A moment later there appeared beyond the grating of the cell door the commander of the Colosseum guards, who had accompanied Fastus and who had stood between the prince and the prisoner.

"Appius Applosus!" exclaimed Maximus Præclarus. "He is no assassin, my friends."

"I am not the assassin of your body, Præclarus," said Applosus, "but I am indeed the assassin of your happiness."

"What do you mean, my friend?" demanded Præclarus.

"In his anger Fastus told me more than he told you."

"He told you what?" asked Præclarus.

"He told me that Dilecta had consented to become his wife only in the hope of saving her father and mother and you, Præclarus, and your mother, Festivitas."

"To call him swine is to insult the swine," said Præclarus. "Take word to her, Applosus, that I would rather die than to see her wed to Fastus."

"She knows that, my friend," said the officer, "but she thinks also of her father and her mother and yours."

Præclarus's chin dropped upon his chest. "I had forgotten that," he moaned. "Oh, there must be some way to stop it."

"He is the son of Cæsar," Applosus reminded him, "and the time is short."

"I know it! I know it!" cried Præclarus, "but it is too hideous. It cannot be."

"This officer is your friend, Præclarus?" asked Tarzan, indicating Appius Applosus.

"Yes," said Præclarus.

"You would trust him fully?" demanded the ape-man.

"With my life and my honor," said Præclarus.

"Tell him where your keys are and let him fetch them," said the ape-man.

Præclarus brightened instantly. "I had not thought of that," he cried, "but no, his life would be in jeopardy."

"It already is," said Applosus. "Fastus will never forget or forgive what I said tonight. You, Præclarus, know that I am already doomed. What keys do you want? Where are they? I will fetch them."

"Perhaps not when you know what they are," said Præclarus.

"I can guess," replied Appius Applosus.

"You have been in my apartments often, Applosus?"

The other nodded affirmatively.

"You recall the shelves near the window where my books lie?"

"Yes."

"The back of the third shelf slides to one side and behind it, in the wall, you will find the keys."

"Good, Præclarus. You shall have them," said the officer.

The others watched the diminishing light as Appius Applosus departed along the corridor beneath the Colosseum.

The last day of the games had come. The bloodthirsty populace had gathered once more as eager and enthusiastic as though they were about to experience a new and unfamiliar thrill, their appetites swept as clean of the memories of the past week as were the fresh sands of the arena of the brown stains of yesterday.

For the last time the inmates of the cell were taken to enclosures nearer to the entrance to the arena. They had fared better, perhaps, than others, for of the twelve rings only four were empty.

Maximus Præclarus alone was left behind. "Good-by," he said. "Those of you who survive the day shall be free. We shall not see one another again. Good luck to you and may the gods give strength and skill to your arms—that is all that I can ask of them, for not even the gods could give you more courage than you already possess."

"Applosus has failed us," said Hasta.

Tarzan looked troubled. "If only you were coming out with us, Præclarus, we should not then need the keys."

From within the enclosure, where they were confined, Tarzan and his companions could hear the sounds of combat and the groans and hoots and applause of the audience, but they could not see the floor of the arena.

It was a very large room with heavily barred windows and a door. Sometimes two men, sometimes four, sometimes six would go out together, but only one, or two, or three returned. The effect upon the nerves of those who remained uncalled was maddening. For some the suspense became almost unendurable. Two attempted suicide and others tried to pick quarrels with their fellow prisoners, but there were many guards within the room and the prisoners were unarmed, their weapons being issued to them only after they had quit the enclosure and were about to enter the arena.

The afternoon was drawing to a close. Metellus had fought with a gladiator, both in full armor. Hasta and Tarzan had heard the excited cries of the populace. They had heard cheer after cheer, which indicated that each man was putting up a skilful and courageous fight. There was an instant of silence and then the loud cries of *"Habet! Habet!"*

"It is over," whispered Cassius Hasta.

Tarzan made no reply. He had grown to like these men, for he had found them brave and simple and loyal and he, too, was inwardly moved by the suspense that must be endured until one or the other returned to the enclosure; but he gave no outward sign of his perturbation, and while Cassius Hasta paced nervously to and fro Tarzan of the Apes stood silently, with folded arms, watching the door. After awhile it opened and Cæcilius Metellus crossed the threshold.

Cassius Hasta uttered a cry of relief and sprang forward to embrace his friend.

Again the door swung open and a minor official entered. "Come," he cried, "all of you. It is the last event."

Outside the enclosure each man was given a sword, dagger, pike, shield, and a hempen net, and one by one, as they were thus equipped, they were sent into the arena. All the survivors of the week of combat were there—one hundred of them.

They were divided into two equal parties, and red ribbons were fastened to the shoulders of one party and white ribbons to the shoulders of the other.

Tarzan was among the reds, as were Hasta, Metellus, Lukedi, Mpingu, and Ogonyo.

"What are we supposed to do?" asked Tarzan of Hasta.

"The reds will fight against the whites until all the reds are killed or all the whites."

"They should see blood enough to suit them now," said Tarzan.

"They can never get enough of it," replied Metellus.

The two parties marched to the opposite end of the arena

and received their instructions from the præfect in charge of the games, and then they were formed, the reds upon one side of the arena, the whites upon the other. Trumpets sounded and the armed men advanced toward one another.

Tarzan smiled to himself as he considered the weapons with which he was supposed to defend himself. The pike he was sure of, for the Waziri are great spearmen and Tarzan excelled even among them, and with the dagger he felt at home, so long had the hunting-knife of his father been his only weapon of protection—but the Spanish sword, he felt, would probably prove more of a liability than an asset, while the net in his hands could be nothing more than a sorry joke. He would like to have thrown his shield aside, for he did not like shields, considering them, as a rule, useless encumbrances, but he had used them before when the Waziri had fought other native tribes, and knowing that they were constructed as a defense against the very weapons that his opponents were using he retained his and advanced with the others toward the white line. He had determined that their only hope lay in accounting for as many of their adversaries in the first clash of arms as was possible, and this word he had passed down the line with the further admonition that the instant that a man had disposed of an antagonist he turn immediately to help the red nearest him, or the one most sorely beset.

As the two lines drew closer, each man selected the opponent opposite him and Tarzan found that he faced a warrior from the outer villages. They came closer. Some of the men, more eager or nervous than the others, were in advance; some, more fearful, lagged behind. Tarzan's opponent came upon him. Already pikes were flying through the air. Tarzan and the warrior hurled their missiles at the same instant, and back of the ape-man's throw was all the skill and all the muscle and all the weight that he could command. Tarzan struck upward with his shield and his opponent's pike struck it a glancing blow, but with such force that the spear haft was shattered, while Tarzan's weapon passed through the shield of his opponent and pierced the fellow's heart.

There were two others down—one killed and one wounded —and the Colosseum was a babble of voices and a bedlam of noise. Tarzan sprang quickly to aid one of his fellows, but another white, who had killed his red opponent, ran to interfere. Tarzan's net annoyed him, so he threw it at a white who was pressing one of the reds and took on his fresh opponent, who had drawn his sword. His adversary was a professional gladiator, a man trained in the use of all his weapons, and Tarzan soon realized that only through great strength and agility might he expect to hold his own with this opponent.

The fellow did not rush. He came in slowly and carefully, feeling out Tarzan. He was cautious because he was an old hand at the business and was imbued with but a single hope —to live. He cared as little for the hoots and jibes of the people as he did for their applause, and he hated Cæsar. He soon discovered that Tarzan was adopting defensive tactics only, but whether this was for the purpose of feeling out his opponent or whether it was part of a plan that would lead up to a sudden and swift surprise, the gladiator could not guess, nor did he care particularly, for he knew that he was master of his weapon and many a corpse had been burned that in life had thought to surprise him.

Judging Tarzan's skill with the sword by his skill with the shield, the gladitor thought that he was pitted against a highly skilled adversary, and he waited patiently for Tarzan to open up his offense and reveal his style. But Tarzan had no style that could be compared with that of the gladiator. What he was awaiting was a lucky chance—the only thing that he felt could assure him victory over this wary and highly skilled swordsman—but the gladiator gave him no openings and he was hoping that one of his companions would be free to come to his assistance, when, suddenly and without warning, a net dropped over his shoulders from behind.

16

C ASSIUS HASTA split the helmet of a burly thief who opposed him, and as he turned to look for a new opponent he saw a white cast a net over Tarzan's head and shoulders from the rear, while the ape-man was engaged with a professional gladiator. Cassius was nearer the gladiator than Tarzan's other opponent and with a cry he hurled himself upon him. Tarzan saw what Cassius Hasta had done and wheeled to face the white who had attacked him from the rear.

The gladiator found Cassius Hasta a very different opponent from Tarzan. Perhaps he was not as skilful with his shield. Perhaps he was not as powerful, but never in all his experience had the gladiator met such a swordsman.

The crowd had been watching Tarzan from the beginning of the event because his great height and his nakedness and his leopard skin marked him from all others. They noted that the first cast of his pike had split the shield of his opponent and dropped him dead and they watched his encounter with the gladiator, which did not please them at all. It was far too slow and they hooted and voiced catcalls. When the white cast the net over him they howled with delight, for they did not know from one day to the next, or from one minute to the next, what their own minds would be the next day or the next minute. They were cruel and stupid, but they were no different from the crowds of any place or any time.

As Tarzan, entangled in the net, turned to face the new menace, the white leaped toward him to finish him with a dagger and Tarzan caught the net with the fingers of both his hands and tore it asunder as though it had been made of paper, but the fellow was upon him in the same instant. The dagger hand struck as Tarzan seized the dagger wrist. Blood ran from beneath the leopard skin from a wound over Tarzan's heart, so close had he been to death, but his hand stopped the other just in time and now steel fingers closed upon that wrist until the man cried out with pain as he felt his bones crushed together. The ape-man drew his antagonist toward him and seized him by the throat and shook him as a terrier shakes a rat, while the air trembled to the delighted screams of the mob.

An instant later Tarzan cast the lifeless form aside, picked up his sword and shield that he had been forced to abandon, and sought for new foes. Thus the battle waged around the arena, each side seeking to gain the advantage in numbers so that they might set upon the remnant of their opponents and destroy them. Cassius Hasta had disposed of the gladiator that he had drawn away from Tarzan and was now engaged with another swordsman when a second fell upon him. Two to one are heavy odds, but Cassius Hasta tried to hold the second off until another red could come to his assistance.

This, however, did not conform with the ideas of the whites who were engaging him, and they fell upon him with redoubled fury to prevent the very thing that he hoped for. He saw an opening and quick as lightning his sword leaped into it, severing the jugular vein of one of his antagonists, but his guard was down for the instant and a glancing blow struck his helmet and, though it did not pierce it, it sent him stumbling to the sand, half-stunned.

"*Habet! Habet!*" cried the people, for Cassius Hasta had fallen close to one side of the arena where a great number of people could see him. Standing over him, his antagonist raised his forefinger to the audience and every thumb went down.

With a smile the white raised his sword to drive it through Hasta's throat, but as he paused an instant, facing the crowd, in a little play to the galleries for effect, Tarzan leaped across the soft sand, casting aside his sword and shield, reverting to the primitive, to the beast, to save his friend.

It was like the charge of a lion. The crowd saw and was frozen into silence. They saw him spring in his stride several yards before he reached the opposing gladiator and, like a jungle beast, fall upon the shoulders and back of his prey.

Down the two went across the body of Hasta, but instantly the ape-man was upon his feet and in his hands was his antagonist. He shook him as he had shaken the other—shook him into unconsciousness, choking him as he shook, shook him to death, and cast his body from him.

The crowd went wild. They stood upon their benches and shrieked and waved scarfs and helmets and threw many flowers and sweetmeats into the arena. Tarzan stooped and lifted Cassius Hasta to his feet as he saw that he was not killed and consciousness was returning.

Scanning the arena quickly, he saw that fifteen reds survived and but ten whites. This was a battle for survival. There were no rules and no ethics. It was your life or mine and Tarzan gathered the surplus five and set upon the strongest white, who now, surrounded by six swordsmen, went down to death in an instant.

At Tarzan's command the six divided and each three charged another white with the result that by following these tactics the event was brought to a sudden and bloody close with fifteen reds surviving and the last white slain.

The crowd was crying Tarzan's name above all others, but Sublatus was enraged. The affront that had been put upon him by this wild barbarian had not been avenged as he had hoped, but instead Tarzan had achieved a personal popularity far greater than his own. That it was ephemeral and subject to the changes of the fickle public mind did not lessen the indignation and chagrin of the Emperor. His mind could entertain but one thought toward Tarzan. The creature must be destroyed. He turned to the præfect in charge of the games and whispered a command.

The crowd was loudly demanding that the laurel wreaths be accorded the victors and that they be given their freedom, but instead they were herded back to their enclosure, all but Tarzan.

Perhaps, suggested some members of the audience, Sublatus is going to honor him particularly, and this rumor ran quickly through the crowd, as rumors will, until it became a conviction.

Slaves came and dragged away the corpses of the slain and picked up the discarded weapons and scattered new sand and raked it, while Tarzan stood where he had been told to stand, beneath the loge of Cæsar.

He stood with folded arms, grimly waiting for what he knew not, and then a low groan rose from the crowded stands—a groan that grew in volume to loud cries of anger above which Tarzan caught words that sounded like "Tyrant!" "Coward!" "Traitor!" and "Down with Sublatus!" He looked around and saw them pointing to the opposite end of the arena and, facing in that direction, he saw the thing that had aroused their wrath, for instead of a laurel wreath and freedom there stood eying him a great, black-maned lion, gaunt with hunger.

Toward the anger of the populace Sublatus exhibited, outwardly, an arrogant and indifferent mien. Contemptuously he permitted his gaze to circle the stands, but he whispered orders that sent three centuries of legionaries among the audience in time to overawe a few agitators who would have led them against the imperial loge.

But now the lion was advancing, and the cruel and selfish audience forgot its momentary anger against injustice in the expected thrill of another bloody encounter. Some, who, a moment before, had been loudly acclaiming Tarzan now cheered the lion, though if the lion were vanquished they would again cheer Tarzan. That, however, they did not anticipate, but believed that they had taken sides with the assured winner, since Tarzan was armed only with a dagger, not having recovered his other weapons after he had thrown them aside.

Naked, but for loincloth and leopard skin, Tarzan presented a magnificent picture of physical perfection, and the people of Castra Sanguinarius gave him their admiration, while they placed their denarii and their talents upon the lion.

They had seen other men that week face other lions bravely and hopelessly and they saw the same courageous bearing in the giant barbarian, but the hopelessness they took for granted the ape-man did not feel. With head flattened, half-crouching, the lion moved slowly toward its prey, the tip of its tail twitching in nervous anticipation, its gaunt sides greedy to be filled. Tarzan waited.

Had he been the lion himself, he scarcely could have better known what was passing in that savage brain. He knew to the instant when the final charge would start. He knew the speed of that swift and deadly rush. He knew when and how the lion would rear upon its hind legs to seize him with great talons and mighty, yellow fangs.

He saw the muscles tense. He saw the twitching tail quiet for an instant. His folded arms dropped to his side. The dagger remained in its sheath at his hip. He waited, crouching almost imperceptibly, his weight upon the balls of his feet, and then the lion charged.

Knowing how accurately the beast had timed its final rush, measuring the distance to the fraction of a stride, even as a hunter approaches a jump, the ape-man knew that the surest way in which to gain the first advantage was to disconcert the charging beast by doing that which he would least expect.

Numa the lion knows that his quarry usually does one of two things—he either stands paralyzed with terror or he turns and flees. So seldom does he charge to meet Numa that the lion never takes this possibility into consideration and it was, therefore, this very thing that Tarzan did.

As the lion charged, the ape-man leaped to meet him, and the crowd sat breathless and silent. Even Sublatus leaned forward with parted lips, forgetful, for a moment, that he was Cæsar.

Numa tried to check himself and rear to meet this presumptuous man-thing, but he slipped a little in the sand and the great paw that struck at Tarzan was ill-timed and missed, for the ape-man had dodged to one side and beneath it, and in the fraction of a second that it took Numa to recover himself he found that their positions had been reversed and that the prey that he would have leaped upon had turned swiftly and leaped upon him.

Full upon the back of the lion sprang Tarzan of the Apes. A giant forearm encircled the maned throat; steel-thewed legs crossed beneath the gaunt, slim belly and locked themselves there. Numa reared and pawed and turned to bite the savage beast upon his back, but the vise-like arm about his throat pressed tighter, holding him so that his fangs could not reach their goal. He leaped into the air and when he alighted on the sand shook himself to dislodge the growling man-beast clinging to him.

Holding his position with his legs and one arm, Tarzan, with his free hand, sought the hilt of his dagger. Numa, feeling the life being choked from him, became frantic. He reared upon his hind legs and threw himself upon the ground, rolling upon his antagonist, and now the crowd found its voice again and shouted hoarse delight. Never in the history of the arena had such a contest as this been witnessed. The barbarian was offering such a defense as they had not thought possible and they cheered him, though they knew that even-

119

tually the lion would win. Then Tarzan found his dagger and drove the thin blade into Numa's side, just back of his left elbow. Again and again the knife struck home, but each blow seemed only to increase the savage efforts of the lunging beast to shake the man from his back and tear him to pieces.

Blood was mixed with the foam on Numa's jowls as he stood panting upon trembling legs after a last futile effort to dislodge the ape-man. He swayed dizzily. The knife struck deep again. A great stream of blood gushed from the mouth and nostrils of the dying beast. He lurched forward and fell lifeless upon the crimsoned sand.

Tarzan of the Apes leaped to his feet. The savage personal combat, the blood, the contact with the mighty body of the carnivore had stripped from him the last vestige of the thin veneer of civilization. It was no English Lord who stood there with one foot upon his kill and through narrowed lids glared about him at the roaring populace. It was no man, but a wild beast, that raised its head and voiced the savage victory cry of the bull ape, a cry that stilled the multitude and froze its blood. But, in an instant, the spell that had seized him passed. His expression changed. The shadow of a smile crossed his face as he stooped and, wiping the blood from his dagger upon Numa's mane, returned the weapon to its sheath.

Cæsar's jealousy had turned to terror as he realized the meaning of the tremendous ovation the giant barbarian was receiving from the people of Castra Sanguinarius. He well knew, though he tried to conceal the fact, that he held no place in popular favor and that Fastus, his son, was equally hated and despised.

This barbarian was a friend of Maximus Præclarus, whom he had wronged, and Maximus Præclarus, whose popularity with the troops was second to none, was loved by Dilecta, the daughter of Dion Splendidus, who might easily aspire to the purple with the support of such a popular idol as Tarzan must become if he were given his freedom in accordance with the customs and rules governing the contests. While Tarzan waited in the arena and the people cheered themselves hoarse, more legionaries filed into the stands until the wall bristled with glittering pikes.

Cæsar whispered in consultation with the præfect of the games. Trumpets blared and the præfect arose and raised his open palm for silence. Gradually the din subsided and the people waited, listening, expecting the honors that were customarily bestowed upon the outstanding hero of the games. The præfect cleared his throat.

"This barbarian has furnished such extraordinary entertainment that Cæsar, as a special favor to his loyal subjects, has decided to add one more event to the games in which the barbarian may again demonstrate his supremacy. This event will"—but what further the præfect said was drowned in a murmur of surprise, disapproval, and anger, for the people had sensed by this time the vicious and unfair trick that Sublatus was about to play upon their favorite.

They cared nothing for fair play, for though the individual may prate of it at home it has no place in mob psychology, but the mob knew what it wanted. It wanted to idolize a popular hero. It did not care to see him fight again that day and it wanted to thwart Sublatus, whom it hated. Menacing were the cries and threats directed toward Cæsar, and only the glittering pikes kept the mob at bay.

In the arena the slaves were working rapidly; fallen Numa had been dragged away, the sands swept, and as the last slave disappeared, leaving Tarzan again alone within the enclosure, those menacing gates at the far end swung open once more.

17

A Tarzan looked toward the far end of the arena he saw six bull apes being herded through the gateway. They had heard the victory cry roll thunderously from the arena a few minutes before and they came now from their cages filled with excitement and ferocity. Already had they long been surly and irritable from confinement and from the teasing and baiting to which they had been subjected by the cruel Sanguinarians. Before them they saw a man-thing—a hated Tarmangani. He represented the creatures that had captured them and teased them and hurt them.

"I am Gayat," growled one of the bull apes. "I kill."

"I am Zutho," bellowed another. "I kill."

"Kill the Tarmangani," barked Go-yad, as the six lumbered forward—sometimes erect upon their hind feet, sometimes swinging with gnarled knuckles to the ground.

The crowd hooted and groaned. "Down with Cæsar!" "Death to Sublatus!" rose distinctly above the tumult. To a man they were upon their feet, but the glittering pikes held them in awe as one or two, with more courage than brains, sought to reach the loge of Cæsar, but ended upon the pikes of the legionaries instead. Their bodies, lying in the aisles, served as a warning to the others.

Sublatus turned and whispered to a guest in the imperial loge. "This should be a lesson to all who would dare affront Cæsar," he said.

"Quite right," replied the other. "Glorious Cæsar is, indeed, all powerful," but the fellow's lips were blue from terror as he saw how great and menacing was the crowd and how slim and few looked the glittering pikes that stood between it and the imperial loge.

As the apes approached, Zutho was in the lead. "I am Zutho," he cried. "I kill."

"Look well, Zutho, before you kill your friend," replied the ape-man. "I am Tarzan of the Apes."

Zutho stopped, bewildered. The others crowded about him.

"The Tarmangani spoke in the language of the great apes," said Zutho.

"I know him," said Go-yad. "He was king of the tribe when I was a young ape."

"It is, indeed, Whiteskin," said Gayat.

"Yes," said Tarzan, "I am Whiteskin. We are all prisoners here together. These Tarmangani are my enemies and yours. They wish us to fight, but we shall not."

"No," said Zutho, "we shall not fight against Tarzan."

"Good," said the ape-man, as they gathered close around him, sniffing that their noses might validate the testimony of their eyes.

"What has happened?" growled Sublatus. "Why do they not attack him?"

"He has cast a spell upon them," replied Cæsar's guest.

The people looked on wonderingly. They heard the beasts and the man growling at one another. How could they guess that they were speaking together in their common language? They saw Tarzan turn and walk toward Cæsar's loge, his bronzed skin brushing against the black coats of the savage beasts lumbering at his side. The ape-man and the apes halted below imperial Cæsar. Tarzan's eyes ran quickly around the arena. The wall was lined with legionaries so not even Tarzan might pass these unscathed. He looked up at Sublatus.

"Your plan has failed, Cæsar. These that you thought would tear me to pieces are my own people. They will not harm me. If there are any others that you would turn against me let them come now, but be quick, for my patience is growing short and if I should say the word these apes will follow me into the imperial loge and tear you to shreds."

And that is exactly what Tarzan would have done had

he not known that while he doubtless could have killed Sublatus his end would come quickly beneath the pikes of the legionaries. He was not sufficiently well versed in the ways of mobs to know that in their present mood the people would have swarmed to protect him and that the legionaries, with few exceptions, would have joined forces with them against the hated tyrant.

What Tarzan wanted particularly was to effect the escape of Cassius Hasta and Cæcilius Metellus simultaneously with his own, so that he might have the advantage of their assistance in his search for Erich von Harben in the Empire of the East; therefore, when the præfect ordered him back to his dungeon he went, taking the apes with him to their cages.

As the arena gates closed behind him he heard again, above the roaring of the populace, the insistent demand: "Down with Sublatus!"

As the jailer opened the cell door, Tarzan saw that its only occupant was Maximus Præclarus.

"Welcome, Tarzan!" cried the Roman. "I had not thought to see you again. How is it that you are neither dead nor free?"

"It is the justice of Cæsar," replied Tarzan, with a smile, "but at least our friends are free, for I see they are not here."

"Do not deceive yourself, barbarian," said the jailer. "Your friends are chained safely in another cell."

"But they won their freedom," exclaimed Tarzan.

"And so did you," returned the jailer, with a grin; "but are you free?"

"It is an outrage," cried Præclarus. "It cannot be done." The jailer shrugged. "But it is already done," he said.

"And why?" demanded Præclarus.

"Think you that a poor soldier has the confidence of Cæsar?" asked the jailer; "but I have heard the reason rumored. Sedition is in the air. Cæsar fears you and all your friends because the people favor you and you favor Dion Splendidus."

"I see," said Præclarus, "and so we are to remain here indefinitely."

"I should scarcely say indefinitely," grinned the jailer, as he closed the door and locked it, leaving them alone.

"I did not like the look in his eye nor the tone of his voice," said Præclarus, after the fellow was out of hearing. "The gods are unkind, but how can I expect else from them when even my best friend fails me?"

"You mean Appius Applosus?" asked Tarzan.

"None other," replied Præclarus. "If he had fetched the keys, we might yet escape."

"Perhaps we shall in any event," said Tarzan. "I should never give up hope until I were dead—and I have never been dead."

"You do not know either the power or perfidy of Cæsar," replied the Roman.

"Nor does Cæsar know Tarzan of the Apes."

Darkness had but just enveloped the city, blotting out even the dim light of their dungeon cell, when the two men perceived wavering light beams lessening the darkness of the corridor without. The light increased and they knew that someone was approaching, lighting his way with a flaring torch.

Visitors to the dungeon beneath the Colosseum were few in the daytime. Guards and jailers passed occasionally and twice each day slaves came with food, but at night the silent approach of a single torch might more surely augur ill than well. Præclarus and Tarzan dropped the desultory conversation with which they had been whiling away the time and waited in silence for whoever might be coming.

Perhaps the night-time visitor was not for them, but the egotism of misfortune naturally suggested that he was and that his intentions might be more sinister than friendly. But they had not long to wait and their suspicions precluded any possibility of surprise when a man halted before the barred gateway to their cell. As the visitor fitted the key to the lock Præclarus recognized him through the bars.

"Appius Applosus!" he cried. "You have come!'

"Ps-st!" cautioned Applosus, and quickly opening the gate he stepped within and closed it silently behind him. With a quick glance he surveyed the cell and then extinguished his torch against the stone wall. "It is fortunate that you are alone," he said, speaking in whispers, as he dropped to the floor close to the two men.

"You are trembling," said Præclarus. "What has happened?"

"It is not what has happened but what is about to happen that alarms me," replied Applosus. "You have probably wondered why I had not brought the keys. You have doubtless thought me faithless, but the fact is that up to this instant it has been impossible, although I have stood ready before to risk my life in the attempt, even as I am now doing."

"But why should it be so difficult for the commander of the Colosseum guard to visit the dungeon?"

"I am no longer the commander of the guards," replied Applosus. "Something must have aroused Cæsar's suspicions, for I was removed in the hour that I last left you. Whether someone overheard and reported our plan or

124

whether it was merely my known friendship for you that aroused his misgivings, I may only surmise, but the fact remains that I have been kept on duty constantly at the Porta Prætoria since I was transferred there from the Colosseum. I have not even been permitted to return to my home, the reason given being that Cæsar expects an uprising of the barbarians of the outer villages, which, as we all know, is utterly ridiculous.

"I risked everything to leave my post only an hour ago and that because of a word of gossip that was passed to me by a young officer, who came to relieve another at the gate."

"What said he?" demanded Præclarus.

"He said that an officer of the palace guard had told him that he had been ordered to come to your cell tonight and assassinate both you and this white barbarian. I hastened to Festivitas and together we found the keys that I promised to bring you, but even as I slunk through the shadows of the city's streets, endeavoring to reach the Colosseum unobserved or unrecognized, I feared that I might be too late, for Cæsar's orders are that you are to be dispatched at once. Here are the keys, Præclarus. If I may do more, command me."

"No, my friend," replied Præclarus, "you have already risked more than enough. Go at once. Return to your post lest Cæsar learn and destroy you."

"Farewell then and good luck," said Applosus. "If you would leave the city, remember that Appius Applosus commands the Porta Prætoria."

"I shall not forget, my friend," replied Præclarus, "but I shall not impose further risks upon your friendship."

Appius Applosus turned to leave the cell, but he stopped suddenly at the gate. "It is too late," he whispered. "Look!" The faint gleams of distant torch-light were cutting the gloom of the corridor.

"They come!" whispered Præclarus. "Make haste!" but instead Appius Applosus stepped quickly to one side of the doorway, out of sight of the corridor beyond, and drew his Spanish sword.

Rapidly the torch swung down the corridor. The scraping of sandals on stone could be distinctly heard, and the apeman knew that whoever came was alone. A man wrapped in a long dark cloak halted before the barred door and, holding his torch above his head, peered within.

"Maximus Præclarus!" he whispered. "Are you within?"

"Yes," replied Præclarus.

"Good!" exclaimed the other. "I was not sure that this was the right cell."

"What is your errand?" demanded Præclarus.

"I come from Cæsar," said the other. "He sends a note."

"A sharp one?" inquired Præclarus.

"Sharp and pointed," laughed the officer.

"We are expecting you."

"You knew?" demanded the other.

"We guessed, for we know Cæsar."

"Then make your peace with your gods," said the officer, drawing his sword and pushing the door open, "for you are about to die."

There was a cold smile upon his lips as he stepped across the threshold, for Cæsar knew his men and had chosen well the proper type for this deed—a creature without conscience whose envy and jealousy Præclarus had aroused, and the smile was still upon his lips as the sword of Appius Applosus crashed through his helmet to his brain. As the man lunged forward dead, the torch fell from his left hand and was extinguished upon the floor.

"Now go," whispered Præclarus to Applosus, "and maybe the gratitude of those you have saved prove a guard against disaster."

"It could not have turned out better," whispered Applosus. "You have the keys; you have his weapons, and now you have ample time to make your escape before the truth is learned. Good-by, again. Good-by, and may the gods protect you."

As Applosus moved cautiously along the dark corridor, Maximus Præclarus fitted keys to their manacles and both men stood erect, freed at last from their hated chains. No need to formulate plans—they had talked and talked of nothing else for weeks, changing them only to meet altered conditions. Now their first concern was to find Hasta and Metellus and the others upon whose loyalty they could depend and to gather around them as many of the other prisoners as might be willing to follow them in the daring adventure they contemplated.

Through the darkness of the corridor they crept from cell to cell and in the few that still held prisoners they found none unwilling to pledge his loyalty to any cause or to any leader that might offer freedom. Lukedi, Mpingu, and Ogonyo were among those they liberated. They had almost given up hope of finding the others when they came upon Metellus and Hasta in a cell close to the entrance to the arena. With them were a number of professional gladiators, who should have been liberated with the other victors at the end of the games, but who were being kept because of some whim of Cæsar that they could not understand and that only inflamed them to anger against the Emperor.

To a man they pledged themselves to follow wherever Tarzan might lead.

"Few of us will come through alive," said the ape-man, when they had all gathered in the large room that was reserved for the contestants before they were ushered into the arena, "but those who do will have been avenged upon Cæsar for the wrongs that he has done them."

"The others will be welcomed by the gods as heroes worthy of every favor," added Præclarus.

"We do not care whether your cause be right or wrong, or whether we live or die," said a gladiator, "so long as there is good fighting."

"There will be good fighting. I can promise you that," said Tarzan, "and plenty of it."

"Then lead on," said the gladiator.

"But first I must liberate the rest of my friends," said the ape-man.

"We have emptied every cell," said Præclarus. "There are no more."

"Oh, yes, my friend," said Tarzan. "There are still others —the great apes."

18

IN the dungeons of Validus Augustus in Castrum Mare, Erich von Harben and Mallius Lepus awaited the triumph of Validus Augustus and the opening of the games upon the morrow.

"We have nothing to expect but death," said Lepus, gloomily. "Our friends are in disfavor, or in prison, or in exile. The jealousy of Validus Augustus against his nephew, Cassius Hasta, has been invoked against us by Fulvus Fupus to serve his own aims."

"And the fault is mine," said von Harben.

"Do not reproach yourself," replied his friend. "That Favonia gave you her love cannot be held against you. It is only the jealous and scheming mind of Fupus that is to blame."

"My love has brought sorrow to Favonia and disaster to her friends," said von Harben, "and here am I, chained to a stone wall, unable to strike a blow in her defense or theirs."

"Ah, if Cassius Hasta were but here!" exclaimed Lepus. "There is a man. With Fupus adopted by Cæsar, the whole city would arise against Validus Augustus if Cassius Hasta were but here to lead us."

And as they conversed sadly and hopelessly in the dungeons of Castrum Mare, noble guests gathered in the throne-room of Sublatus in the city of Castra Sanguinarius, at the opposite end of the valley. There were senators in rich robes and high officers of the court and of the army, resplendent in jewels and embroidered linen, who, with their wives and their daughters, formed a gorgeous, and glittering company in the pillared chamber, for Fastus, the son of Cæsar, was to wed the daughter of Dion Splendidus that evening.

In the avenue, beyond the palace gates, a great crowd had assembled—a multitude of people pushing and surging to and fro, but pressing ever upon the gates up to the very pikes of the legionaries. It was a noisy crowd—noisy with a deep-throated roar of anger.

"Down with the tyrant!" "Death to Sublatus!" "Death to Fastus!" was the burden of their hymn of hate.

The menacing notes filled the palace, reaching to the throne-room, but the haughty patricians pretended not to hear the voice of the cattle. Why should they fear? Had not Sublatus distributed donations to all the troops that very day? Would not the pikes of the legionaries protect the source of their gratuity? It would serve the ungrateful populace right if Sublatus set the legions upon them, for had he not given them such a pageant and such a week of games as Castra Sanguinarius never had known before?

For the rabble without, their contempt knew no bounds now that they were within the palace of the Emperor, but they did not speak among themselves of the fact that most of them had entered by a back gate after the crowd had upset the litter of a noble senator and spilled its passengers into the dust of the avenue.

With pleasure they anticipated the banquet that would follow the marriage ceremony, and while they laughed and chattered over the gossip of the week, the bride sat stark and cold in an upper chamber of the palace surrounded by her female slaves and comforted by her mother.

"It shall not be," she said. "I shall never be the wife of Fastus," and in the folds of her flowing robe she clutched the hilt of a slim dagger.

In the corridor beneath the Colosseum, Tarzan marshaled his forces. He summoned Lukedi and a chief of one of the outer villages, who had been a fellow prisoner with him and with whom he had fought shoulder to shoulder in the games.

"Go to the Porta Prætoria," he said, "and ask Appius

Applosus to pass you through the city wall as a favor to Maximus Præclarus. Go then among the villages and gather warriors. Tell them that if they would be avenged upon Cæsar and free to live their own lives in their own way, they must rise now and join the citizens who are ready to revolt and destroy the tyrant. Hasten, there is no time to be lost. Gather them quickly and lead them into the city by the Porta Prætoria, straight to the palace of Cæsar."

Warning their followers to silence, Tarzan and Maximus Præclarus led them in the direction of the barracks of the Colosseum guard, where were quartered the men of Præclarus's own cohort.

It was a motley throng of near-naked warriors from the outer villages, slaves from the city, and brown half-castes, among whom were murderers, thieves and professional gladiators. Præclarus and Hasta and Metellus and Tarzan led them, and swarming close to Tarzan were Gayat, Zutho, and Go-yad and their three fellow apes.

Ogonyo was certain now that Tarzan was a demon, for who else might command the hairy men of the woods? Doubtless in each of these fierce bodies presided the ghost of some great Bagego chief. If little Nkima had been the ghost of his grandfather, then these must be the ghosts of very great men, indeed. Ogonyo did not press too closely to these savage allies, nor as a matter of fact did any of the others—not even the most ferocious of the gladiators.

At the barracks Maximus Præclarus knew to whom to speak and what to say, for mutiny had long been rife in the ranks of the legionaries. Only their affection for some of their officers, among whom was Præclarus, had kept them thus long in leash, and now they welcomed the opportunity to follow the young patrician to the very gates of Cæsar's palace.

Following a plan that had been decided upon, Præclarus dispatched a detachment under an officer to the Porta Prætoria with orders to take it by force, if they could not persuade Appius Applosus to join them, and throw it open to the warriors from the outer villages when they should arrive.

Along the broad Via Principalis, overhung by giant trees that formed a tunnel of darkness in the night, Tarzan of the Apes led his followers toward the palace in the wake of a few torch-bearers, who lighted the way.

As they approached their goal, someone upon the outskirts of the crowd, pressing the palace guard, was attracted by the light of their torches and quickly the word was passed that Cæsar had sent for reënforcements—that more troops were coming. The temper of the crowd, already inflamed, was not improved as this news spread quickly through its ranks. A few, following a self-appointed leader, moved forward menacingly to meet the newcomers.

"Who comes?" shouted one.

"It is I, Tarzan of the Apes," replied the ape-man.

The shout that went up in response to this declaration proved that the fickle populace had not, as yet, turned against him.

Within the palace the cries of the people brought a scowl to the face of Cæsar and a sneer to many a patrician lip, but their reaction might have been far different had they known the cause of the elation of the mob.

"Why are you here?" cried voices. "What are you going to do?"

"We have come to rescue Dilecta from the arms of Fastus and to drag the tyrant from the throne of Castra Sanguinarius."

Roars of approval greeted the announcement. "Death to the tyrant!" "Down with the palace guards!" "Kill them!" "Kill them!" rose from a thousand lips.

The crowd pushed forward. The officer of the guard, seeing the reënforcements, among which were many legionaries, ordered his men to fall back within the palace grounds and close and bar the gate, nor did they succeed in accomplishing this an instant too soon, for as the bolts were shot the crowd hurled itself upon the stout barriers of iron and oak.

A pale-faced messenger hastened to the throne-room and to Cæsar's side.

"The people have risen," he whispered, hoarsely, "and many soldiers and gladiators and slaves have joined them. They are throwing themselves against the gates, which cannot hold for long."

Cæsar arose and paced nervously to and fro, and presently he paused and summoned officers.

"Dispatch messengers to every gate and every barracks," he ordered. "Summon the troops to the last man that may be spared from the gates. Order them to fall upon the rabble and kill. Let them kill until no citizen remains alive in the streets of Castra Sanguinarius. Take no prisoners."

As word finds its way through a crowd, as though by some strange telepathic means, so the knowledge soon became common that Sublatus had ordered every legionary in the city to the palace with instructions to destroy the revolutionaries to the last man.

The people, encouraged by the presence of the legionaries led by Præclarus, had renewed their assaults upon the gates, and though many were piked through its bars, their bodies were dragged away by their friends and others took their places, so that the gates sagged and bent beneath their numbers; yet they held and Tarzan saw that they might hold for long—or at least long enough to permit the arrival of the reënforcements that, if they remained loyal to Cæsar, might overcome this undisciplined mob with ease.

Gathering around him some of those he knew best, Tarzan explained a new plan that was greeted with exclamations of approval, and summoning the apes he moved down the dark avenue, followed by Maximus Præclarus, Cassius Hasta, Cæcilius Metellus, Mpingu, and a half dozen of Castra Sanguinarius's most famous gladiators.

The wedding of Fastus and Dilecta was to take place upon the steps of Cæsar's throne. The high priest of the temple stood facing the audience, and just below him, and at one side, Fastus waited, while slowly up the center of the long chamber came the bride, followed by the vestal virgins, who tended the temple's sacred fires.

Dilecta was pale, but she did not falter as she moved slowly forward to her doom. There were many who whispered that she looked the Empress already, so noble was her mien, so stately her carriage. They could not see the slim dagger clutched in her right hand beneath the flowing bridal robes. Up the aisle she moved, but she did not halt before the priest as Fastus had done—and as she should have done—but passed him and mounting the first few steps toward the throne she halted, facing Sublatus.

"The people of Castra Sanguinarius have been taught through all the ages that they may look to Cæsar for protection," she said. "Cæsar not only makes the law—he is the law. He is either the personification of justice or he is a tyrant. Which, Sublatus, are you?"

Cæsar flushed. "What mad whim is this, child?" he demanded. "Who has set you to speak such words to Cæsar?"

"I have not been prompted," replied the girl, wearily. "It is my last hope and though I knew beforehand that it was futile, I felt that I must not cast it aside as useless before putting it to the test."

"Come! Come!" snapped Cæsar. "Enough of this foolishness. Take your place before the priest and repeat your marriage vows."

"You cannot refuse me," cried the girl, stubbornly. "I appeal to Cæsar, which is my right as a citizen of Rome, the mother city that we have never seen, but whose right to citizenship has been handed down to us from our ancient sires. Unless the spark of freedom is to be denied us, you cannot refuse me that right, Sublatus."

The Emperor paled and then flushed with anger. "Come

to me tomorrow," he said. "You shall have whatever you wish."

"If you do not hear me now, there will be no tomorrow," she said. "I demand my rights now."

"Well," demanded Cæsar, coldly, "what favor do you seek?"

"I seek no favor," replied Dilecta. "I seek the right to know if the thing for which I am paying this awful price has been done, as it was promised."

"What do you mean?" demanded Sublatus. "What proof do you wish?"

"I wish to see Maximus Præclarus here alive and free," replied the girl, "before I pledge my troth to Fastus. That, as you well know, was the price of my promise to wed him."

Cæsar arose angrily. "That cannot be," he said.

"Oh, yes, it can be," cried a voice from the balcony at the side of the chamber, "for Maximus Præclarus stands just behind me."

19

EVERY eye turned in the direction of the balcony from which came the voice of the speaker. A gasp of astonishment arose from the crowded room.

"The barbarian!" "Maximus Præclarus!" cried a score of voices.

"The guard! The guard!" screamed Cæsar, as Tarzan leaped from the balcony to one of the tall pillars that supported the roof and slid quickly to the floor, while behind him came six hairy apes.

A dozen swords flashed from their scabbards as Tarzan and the six leaped toward the throne. Women screamed and fainted. Cæsar shrank back upon his golden seat, momentarily paralyzed by terror.

A noble with bared blade leaped in front of Tarzan to bar his way, but Go-yad sprang full upon him. Yellow fangs bit once into his neck and, as the great ape arose and standing on the body of his kill roared forth his victory cry, the other nobles shrank back. Fastus, with a scream, turned and fled, and Tarzan leaped to Dilecta's side. As the apes ascended the steps to the dais, Cæsar, jabbering with terror,

132

scuttled from his seat and hid, half-fainting, behind the great throne that was the symbol of his majesty and his power.

But it was not long before the nobles and officers and soldiers in the apartment regained the presence of mind that the sudden advent of this horrid horde had scattered to the four winds, and now, seeing only the wild barbarian and six unarmed beasts threatening them, they pushed forward. Just then a small door beneath the balcony from which Tarzan had descended to the floor of the throne-room was pushed open, giving entrance to Maximus Præclarus, Cassius Hasta, Cæcilius Metellus, Mpingu, and the others who had accompanied Tarzan over the palace wall beneath the shadows of the great trees into which the ape-man and the apes had assisted their less agile fellows.

As Cæsar's defenders sprang forward they were met by some of the best swords in Castra Sanguinarius, as in the forefront of the fighting were the very gladiators whose exploits they had cheered during the week. Tarzan passed Dilecta to Mpingu, for he and Præclarus must lend a hand in the fighting.

Slowly, Dilecta's defenders fell back before the greater number of nobles, soldiers, and guardsmen who were summoned from other parts of the palace. Back toward the little door they fell, while shoulder to shoulder with the gladiators and with Maximus Præclarus and Hasta and Metellus, Tarzan fought and the great apes spread consternation among all because of their disposition to attack friend as well as foe.

And out upon the Via Principalis the crowd surged and the great gates gave to a shrieking mob that poured into the palace grounds, overwhelming the guards, trampling them —trampling their own dead and their own living.

But the veteran legionaries who composed the palace guard made a new stand at the entrance to the palace. Once more they checked the undisciplined rabble, which had by now grown to such proportions that the revolting troops, who had joined them, were lost in their midst. The guard had dragged an onager to the palace steps and were discharging stones into the midst of the crowd, which continued to rush forward to fall upon the pikes of the palace defenders.

In the distance trumpets sounded from the direction of the Porta Decumana, and from the Porta Principalis Dextra came the sound of advancing troops. At first those upon the outskirts of the mob, who had heard these sounds, did not interpret them correctly. They cheered and shouted. These cowards that hang always upon the fringe of every crowd, letting others take the risks and do the fighting for them,

133

thought that more troops had revolted and that the reënforcements were for them. But their joy was short-lived, for the first century that swung into the Via Principalis from the Porta Decumana fell upon them with pike and sword until those who were not slain escaped, screaming, in all directions.

Century after century came at the double. They cleared the Via Principalis and fell upon the mob within the palace court until the revolt dissolved into screaming individuals fleeing through the darkness of the palace grounds, seeking any shelter that they might find, while terrible legionaries pursued them with flaming torches and bloody swords.

Back into the little room from which they had come fell Tarzan and his followers. The doorway was small and it was not difficult for a few men to hold it, but when they would have retreated through the window they had entered and gone back into the palace grounds to seek escape across the walls in the shadows of the old trees, they saw the grounds swarming with legionaries and realized that the back of the revolt had been broken.

The anteroom in which they had taken refuge would barely accomodate them all, but it offered probably the best refuge they could have found in all the palace of Sublatus, for there were but two openings in it—the single small doorway leading into the throne-room and an even smaller window letting into the palace gardens. The walls were all stone and proof against any weapons at the disposal of the legionaries; yet if the uprising had failed and the legionaries had not joined the people, as they had expected, of what value this temporary sanctuary? The instant that hunger and thirst assailed them this same room would become their prison cell and torture chamber—and perhaps for many of them a vestibule to the grave.

"Ah, Dilecta," cried Præclarus, in the first moment that he could seize to go to her side, "I have found you only to lose you again. My rashness, perhaps, has brought you death."

"Your coming saved me from death," replied the girl, drawing the dagger from her gown and exhibiting it to Præclarus. "I chose this as husband rather than Fastus," she said, "so if I die now I have lived longer than I should have, had you not come; and at least I die happy, for we shall die together."

"This is no time to be speaking of dying," said Tarzan. "Did you think a few hours ago that you would ever be together again? Well, here you are. Perhaps in a few more hours everything will be changed and you will be laughing at the fears you are now entertaining."

Some of the gladiators, who were standing near and had overheard Tarzan's words, shook their heads.

"Any of us who gets out of this room alive" said one, "will be burned at the stake, or fed to lions, or pulled apart by wild buffalo. We are through, but it has been a good fight, and I for one thank this great barbarian for this glorious end."

Tarzan shrugged and turned away. "I am not dead yet," he said, "and not until I am dead is it time to think of it—and then it will be too late."

Maximus Præclarus laughed. "Perhaps you are right," he said. "What do you suggest? If we stay here, we shall be slain, so you must have some plan for getting us out."

"If we can discern no hope of advantage through our own efforts," replied Tarzan, "we must look elsewhere and await such favors of fortune as may come from without, either through the intervention of our friends beyond the palace grounds or from the carelessness of the enemy himself. I admit that just at present our case appears desperate, but even so I am not without hope; at least we may be cheered by the realization that whatever turn events may take it must be for the better, since nothing could be worse."

"I do not agree with you," said Metellus, pointing through the window. "See, they are setting up a small ballista in the garden. Presently our condition will be much worse than it is now."

"The walls appear substantial," returned the ape-man. "Do you think they can batter them down, Præclarus?"

"I doubt it," replied the Roman, "but every missile that comes through the window must take its toll, as we are so crowded here that all of us cannot get out of range."

The legionaries that had been summoned to the throne-room had been held at the small doorway by a handful of gladiators and the defenders had been able to close and bar the stout oaken door. For a time there had been silence in the throne-room and no attempt was made to gain entrance to the room upon that side; while upon the garden side two or three attempts to rush the window had been thwarted, and now the legionaries held off while the small ballista was being dragged into place and trained upon the palace wall.

Dilecta having been placed in an angle of the room where she would be safest, Tarzan and his lieutenants watched the operations of the legionaries in the garden.

"They do not seem to be aiming directly at the window," remarked Cassius Hasta.

"No," said Præclarus. "I rather think they intend making a breach in the wall through which a sufficient number of them can enter to overpower us."

"If we could rush the ballista and take it," mused Tarzan, "we could make it rather hot for them. Let us hold ourselves in readiness for that, if their missiles make it too hot for us in here. We shall have some advantage if we anticipate their assault by a sortie of our own."

A dull thud upon the door at the opposite end of the room brought the startled attention of the defenders to that quarter. The oak door sagged and the stone walls trembled to the impact.

Cassius Hasta smiled wryly. "They have brought a ram," he said.

And now a heavy projectile shook the outer wall and a piece of plaster crumbled to the floor upon the inside—the ballista had come into action. Once again the heavy battering-ram shivered the groaning timbers of the door and the inmates of the room could hear the legionaries chanting the hymn of the ram to the cadence of which they swung it back and heaved it forward.

The troops in the garden went about their duty with quiet, military efficiency. Each time a stone from the ballista struck the wall there was a shout, but there was nothing spontaneous in the demonstration, which seemed as perfunctory as the mechanical operation of the ancient war-engine that delivered its missiles with almost clocklike regularity.

The greatest damage that the ballista appeared to be doing was to the plaster on the inside of the wall, but the battering-ram was slowly but surely shattering the door at the opposite side of the room.

"Look," said Metellus, "they are altering the line of the ballista. They have discovered that they can effect nothing against the wall."

"They are aiming at the window," said Præclarus.

"Those of you who are in line with the window lie down upon the floor," commanded Tarzan. "Quickly! the hammer is falling upon the trigger."

The next missile struck one side of the window, carrying away a piece of the stone, and this time the result was followed by an enthusiastic shout from the legionaries in the garden.

"That's what they should have done in the beginning," commented Hasta. "If they get the walls started at the edge of the window, they can make a breach more quickly there than elsewhere."

"That is evidently what they are planning on doing," said Metellus, as a second missile struck in the same place and a large fragment of the wall crumbled.

"Look to the door," shouted Tarzan, as the weakened timbers sagged to the impact of the ram.

A dozen swordsmen stood ready and waiting to receive the legionaries, whose rush they expected the instant that the door fell. At one side of the room the six apes crouched, growling, and kept in leash only by the repeated assurances of Tarzan that the man-things in the room with them were the friends of the ape-man.

As the door crashed, there was a momentary silence, as each side waited to see what the other would do, and in the lull that ensued there came through the air a roaring sound ominous and threatening, and then the shouts of the legionaries in the throne-room and the legionaries in the garden drowned all other sounds.

The gap around the window had been enlarged. The missiles of the ballista had crumbled the wall from the ceiling to the floor, and as though in accordance with a prearranged plan the legionaries assaulted simultaneously, one group rushing the doorway from the throne-room, the other the breach in the opposite wall.

Tarzan turned toward the apes and pointing in the direction of the breached wall, shouted: "Stop them, Zutho! Kill, Go-yad! Kill!"

The men near him looked at him in surprise and perhaps they shuddered a little as they heard the growling voice of a beast issue from the throat of the giant barbarian, but instantly they realized he was speaking to his hairy fellows, as they saw the apes spring forward with bared fangs and, growling hideously, throw themselves upon the first legionaries to reach the window. Two apes went down, pierced by Roman pikes, but before the beastly rage of the others Cæsar's soldiers gave back.

"After them," cried Tarzan to Præclarus. "Follow them into the garden. Capture the ballista and turn it upon the legionaries. We will hold the throne-room door until you have seized the ballista, then we shall fall back upon you."

After the battling apes rushed the three patricians, Maximus Præclarus, Cassius Hasta, and Cæcilius Metellus, leading gladiators, thieves, murderers, and slaves into the garden, profiting by the temporary advantage the apes had gained for them.

Side by side with the remaining gladiators Tarzan fought to hold the legionaries back from the little doorway until the balance of his party had won safely to the garden and seized the ballista. Glancing back he saw Mpingu leading Dilecta from the room in the rear of the escaped prisoners. Then he turned again to the defense of the doorway, which his little party held stubbornly until Tarzan saw the ballista in the hands of his own men, and, giving step by step across the room, he and they backed through the breach in the wall.

At a shout of command from Præclarus, they leaped to one side. The hammer fell upon the trigger of the ballista, which Præclarus had lined upon the window, and a heavy rock drove full into the faces of the legionaries.

For a moment the fates had been kind to Tarzan and his fellows, but it soon became apparent that they were little if any better off here than in the room they had just quitted, for in the garden they were ringed by legionaries. Pikes were flying through the air, and though the ballista and their own good swords were keeping the enemy at a respectful distance, there was none among them who believed that they could for long withstand the superior numbers and the better equipment of their adversaries.

There came a pause in the fighting, which must necessarily be the case in hand-to-hand encounters, and as though by tacit agreement each side rested. The three whites watched the enemy closely. "They are preparing for a concerted attack with pikes," said Præclarus.

"That will write finis to our earthly endeavors," remarked Cassius Hasta.

"May the gods receive us with rejoicing," said Cæcilius Metellus.

"I think the gods prefer them to us," said Tarzan.

"Why?" demanded Cassius Hasta.

"Because they have taken so many more of them to heaven this night," replied the ape-man, pointing at the corpses lying about the garden, and Cassius Hasta smiled, appreciatively.

"They will charge in another moment," said Maximus Præclarus, and turning to Dilecta he took her in his arms and kissed her. "Good-by, dear heart," he said. "How fleeting is happiness! How futile the hopes of mortal man!"

"Not good-by, Præclarus," replied the girl, "for where you go I shall go," and she showed him the slim dagger in her hand.

"No," cried the man. "Promise me that you will not do that."

"And why not? Is not death sweeter than Fastus?"

"Perhaps you are right," he said, sadly.

"They come," cried Cassius Hasta.

"Ready!" shouted Tarzan. "Give them all we have. Death is better than the dungeons of the Colosseum."

20

FROM the far end of the garden, above the din of breaking battle, rose a savage cry—a new note that attracted the startled attention of the contestants upon both sides. Tarzan's head snapped to attention. His nostrils sniffed the air. Recognition, hope, surprise, incredulity surged through his consciousness as he stood there with flashing eyes looking out over the heads of his adversaries.

In increasing volume the savage roar rolled into the garden of Cæsar. The legionaries turned to face the vanguard of an army led by a horde of warriors, glistening giants from whose proud heads floated white feather warbonnets and from whose throats issued the savage war-cry that had filled the heart of Tarzan—the Waziri had come.

At their head Tarzan saw Muviro and with him was Lukedi, but what the ape-man did not see, and what none of those in the garden of Cæsar saw until later, was the horde of warriors from the outer villages of Castra Sanguinarius that, following the Waziri into the city, were already overrunning the palace seeking the vengeance that had so long been denied them.

As the last of the legionaries in the garden threw down their arms and begged Tarzan's protection, Muviro ran to the ape-man and, kneeling at his feet, kissed his hand, and at the same instant a little monkey dropped from an overhanging tree onto Tarzan's shoulder.

"The gods of our ancestors have been good to the Waziri," said Muviro, "otherwise we should have been too late."

"I was puzzled as to how you found me," said Tarzan, "until I saw Nkima."

"Yes, it was Nkima," said Muviro. "He came back to the country of the Waziri, to the land of Tarzan, and led us here. Many times we would have turned back thinking that he was mad, but he urged us on and we followed him, and now the big Bwana can come back with us to the home of his own people."

"No," said Tarzan, shaking his head, "I cannot come yet. The son of my good friend is still in this valley, but you are just in time to help me rescue him, nor is there any time to lose."

Legionaries, throwing down their arms, were running from the palace, from which came the shrieks and groans of the dying and the savage hoots and cries of the avenging horde. Præclarus stepped to Tarzan's side.

"The barbarians of the outer villages are attacking the city, murdering all who fall into their hands," he cried. "We must gather what men we can and make a stand against them. Will these warriors, who have just come, fight with us against them?"

"They will fight as I direct," replied Tarzan, "but I think it will not be necessary to make war upon the barbarians. Lukedi, where are the white officers who command the barbarians?"

"Once they neared the palace," replied Lukedi, "the warriors became so excited that they broke away from their white leaders and followed their own chieftain."

"Go and fetch their greatest chief," directed Tarzan.

During the half hour that followed, Tarzan and his lieutenants were busy reorganizing their forces into which were incorporated the legionaries who had surrendered to them, in caring for the wounded, and planning for the future. From the palace came the hoarse cries of the looting soldiers, and Tarzan had about abandoned hope that Lukedi would be able to persuade a chief to come to him when Lukedi returned, accompanied by two warriors from the outer villages, whose bearing and ornaments proclaimed them chieftains.

"You are the man called Tarzan?" demanded one of the chiefs.

The ape-man nodded. "I am," he said.

"We have been looking for you. This Bagego said that you have promised that no more shall our people be taken into slavery and no longer shall our warriors be condemned to the arena. How can you, who are yourself a barbarian, guarantee this to us?"

"If I cannot guarantee it, you have the power to enforce it yourself," replied the ape-man, "and I with my Waziri will aid you, but now you must gather your warriors. Let no one be killed from now on who does not oppose you. Gather your warriors and take them into the avenue before the palace and then come with your sub-chiefs to the throne-room of Cæsar. There we shall demand and receive justice, not for the moment but for all time. Go!"

Eventually the looting horde was quieted by their chiefs and withdrawn to the Via Principalis. Waziri warriors manned the shattered gate of Cæsar's palace and lined the corridor to the throne-room and the aisle to the foot of the throne. They formed a half circle about the throne itself, and upon the throne of Cæsar sat Tarzan of the Apes with

Pærclarus and Dilecta and Cassius Hasta and Cæcilius Metellus and Muviro about him, while little Nkima sat upon his shoulder and complained bitterly, for Nkima, as usual, was frightened and cold and hungry.

"Send legionaries to fetch Sublatus and Fastus," Tarzan directed Præclarus, "for this business must be attended to quickly, as within the hour I march on Castrum Mare."

Flushed with excitement, the legionaries that had been sent to fetch Sublatus and Fastus rushed into the throne-room. "Sublatus is dead!" they cried. "Fastus is dead! The barbarians have slain them. The chambers and corridors above are filled with the bodies of senators, nobles, and officers of the legion."

"Are none left alive?" demanded Præclarus, paling.

"Yes," replied one of the legionaries, "there were many barricaded in another apartment who withstood the onslaught of the warriors. We explained to them that they are now safe and they are coming to the throne-room," and up the aisle marched the remnants of the wedding guests, the sweat and blood upon the men evidencing the dire straits from which they had been delivered, the women still nervous and hysterical. Leading them came Dion Splendidus, and at sight of him Dilecta gave a cry of relief and pleasure and ran down the steps of the throne and along the aisle to meet him.

Tarzan's face lighted with relief when he saw the old senator, for his weeks in the home of Festivitas and his long incarceration with Maximus Præclarus in the dungeons of the Colosseum had familiarized him with the politics of Castra Sanguinarius, and now the presence of Dion Splendidus was all that he needed to complete the plans that the tyranny and cruelty of Sublatus had forced upon him.

He rose from the throne and raised his hand for silence. The hum of voices ceased. "Cæsar is dead, but upon some-one of you must fall the mantle of Cæsar."

"Long live Tarzan! Long live the new Cæsar!" cried one of the gladiators, and instantly every Sanguinarian in the room took up the cry.

The ape-man smiled and shook his head. "No," he said, "not I, but there is one here to whom I offer the imperial diadem upon the condition that he fulfill the promises I have made to the barbarians of the outer villages.

"Dion Splendidus, will you accept the imperial purple with the understanding that the men of the outer villages shall be forever free; that no longer shall their girls or their boys be pressed into slavery, or their warriors forced to do battle in the arena?" Dion Splendidus bowed his head in assent— and thus did Tarzan refuse the diadem and create a Cæsar.

21

THE yearly triumph of Validus Augustus, Emperor of the East, had been a poor thing by comparison with that of Sublatus of Castra Sanguinarius, though dignity and interest was lent the occasion by the presence of the much-advertised barbarian chieftain, who strode in chains behind Cæsars chariot.

The vain show of imperial power pleased Validus Augustus, deceiving perhaps the more ignorant of his subjects, and would have given Erich von Harben cause for laughter had he not realized the seriousness of his position.

No captive chained to the chariot of the greatest Cæsar that ever lived had faced a more hopeless situation than he. What though he knew that a regiment of marines or a squadron of Uhlans might have reduced this entire empire to vassalage? What though he knew that the mayor of many a modern city could have commanded a fighting force far greater and much more effective than this little Cæsar? The knowledge was only tantalizing, for the fact remained that Validus Augustus was supreme here and there was neither regiment of marines nor squadron of Uhlans to question his behavior toward the subject of a great republic that could have swallowed his entire empire without being conscious of any discomfort. The triumph was over. Von Harben had been returned to the cell that he occupied with Mallius Lepus.

"You are back early," said Lepus. "How did the triumph of Validus impress you?"

"It was not much of a show, if I may judge by the amount of enthusiasm displayed by the people."

"The triumphs of Validus are always poor things," said Lepus. "He would rather put ten talents in his belly or on his back than spend one denarius to amuse the people."

"And the games," asked von Harben, "will they be as poor?"

"They do not amount to much," said Lepus. "We have few criminals here and as we have to purchase all our slaves, they are too valuable to waste in this way. Many of the contests are between wild beasts, an occasional thief or murderer may be pitted against a gladiator, but for the most part

Validus depends upon professional gladiators and political prisoners—enemies or supposed enemies of Cæsar. More often they are like you and I—victims of the lying and jealous intrigues of favorites. There are about twenty such in the dungeons now, and they will furnish the most interesting entertainment of the games."

"And if we are victorious, we are freed?" asked von Harben.

"We shall not be victorious," said Mallius Lepus. "Fulvus Fupus has seen to that, you may rest assured."

"It is terrible," muttered von Harben.

"You are afraid to die?" asked Mallius Lepus.

"It is not that," said von Harben. "I am thinking of Favonia."

"And well you may," said Mallius Lepus. "My sweet cousin would be happier dead than married to Fulvus Fupus."

"I feel so helpless," said von Harben. "Not a friend, not even my faithful body servant, Gabula."

"Oh, that reminds me," exclaimed Lepus. "They were here looking for him this morning."

"Looking for him? Is he not confined in the dungeon?"

"He was, but he was detailed with other prisoners to prepare the arena last night, and during the darkness of early morning he is supposed to have escaped—but be that as it may, they were looking for him."

"Good!" exclaimed von Harben. "I shall feel better just knowing that he is at large, though there is nothing that he can do for me. Where could he have gone?"

"Castrum Mare is ill guarded along its waterfront, but the lake itself and the crocodiles form a barrier as efficacious as many legionaries. Gabula may have scaled the wall, but the chances are that he is hiding within the city, protected by other slaves or, possibly, by Septimus Favonius himself."

"I wish I might feel that the poor, faithful fellow had been able to escape the country and return to his own people," said von Harben.

Mallius Lepus shook his head. "That is impossible," he said. "Though you came down over the cliff, he could not return that way, and even if he could find the pass to the outer world, he would fall into the hands of the soldiers of Castra Sanguinarius or the barbarians of their outer villages. No, there is no chance that Gabula will escape."

The time passed quickly, all too quickly, between the hour that Erich von Harben was returned to his cell, following his exhibition in the triumph of Validus Augustus, and the coming of the Colosseum guards to drive them into the arena.

The Colosseum was packed. The loges of the patricians

were filled. The haughty Cæsar of the East sat upon an ornate throne, shaded by a canopy of purple linen. Septimus Favonius sat with bowed head in his loge and with him was his wife and Favonia. The girl sat with staring eyes fixed upon the gateway from which the contestants were emerging. She saw her cousin, Mallius Lepus, emerge and with him Erich von Harben, and she shuddered and closed her eyes for a moment.

When she opened them again the column was forming and the contestants were marched across the white sands to receive the commands of Cæsar. With Mallius Lepus and von Harben marched the twenty political prisoners, all of whom were of the patrician class. Then came the professional gladiators—coarse, brutal men, whose business it was to kill or be killed. Leading these, with a bold swagger, was one who had been champion gladiator of Castrum Mare for five years. If the people had an idol, it was he. They roared their approval of him. "Claudius Taurus! Claudius Taurus!" rose above a babel of voices. A few mean thieves, some frightened slaves, and a half dozen lions completed the victims that were to make a Roman holiday.

Erich von Harben had often been fascinated by the stories of the games of ancient Rome. Often had he pictured the Colosseum packed with its thousands and the contestants upon the white sand of the arena, but now he realized that they had been but pictures—but the photographs of his imagination. The people in those dreams had been but picture people—automatons, who move only when we look at them. When there had been action on the sand the audience had been a silent etching, and when the audience had roared and turned its thumbs down the actors had been mute and motionless.

How different, this! He saw the constant motion in the packed stands, the mosaic of a thousand daubs of color that became kaleidoscopic with every move of the multitude. He heard the hum of voices and sensed the offensive odor of many human bodies. He saw the hawkers and vendors passing along the aisles shouting their wares. He saw the legionaries stationed everywhere. He saw the rich in their canopied loges and the poor in the hot sun of the cheap seats.

Sweat was trickling down the back of the neck of the patrician marching just in front of him. He glanced at Claudius Taurus. He saw that his tunic was faded and that his hairy legs were dirty. He had always thought of gladiators as clean-limbed and resplendent. Claudius Taurus shocked him.

As they formed in solid rank before the loge of Cæsar, von Harben smelled the men pressing close behind him. The air was hot and oppressive. The whole thing was disgusting.

There was no grandeur to it, no dignity. He wondered if it had been like this in Rome.

And then he looked up into the loge of Cæsar. He saw the man in gorgeous robes, sitting upon his carved throne. He saw naked slaves swaying long-handled fans of feathers above the head of Cæsar. He saw large men in gorgeous tunics and cuirasses of shining gold. He saw the wealth and pomp and circumstance of power, and something told him that after all ancient Rome had probably been much as this was—that its populace had smelled and that its gladiators had had hairy legs with dirt on them and that its patricians had sweated behind the ears.

Perhaps Validus Augustus was as great a Cæsar as any of them, for did he not rule half of his known world? Few of them had done more than this.

His eyes wandered along the row of loges. The præfect of the games was speaking and von Harben heard his voice, but the words did not reach his brain, for his eyes had suddenly met those of a girl.

He saw the anguish and hopeless horror in her face and he tried to smile as he looked at her, a smile of encouragement and hope, but she only saw the beginning of the smile, for the tears came and the image of the man she loved was only a dull blur like the pain in her heart.

A movement in the stands behind the loges attracted von Harben's eyes and he puckered his brows, straining his faculties to assure himself that he must be mistaken, but he was not. What he had seen was Gabula—he was moving toward the imperial loge, where he disappeared behind the hangings that formed the background of Cæsar's throne.

Then the præfect ordered them from the arena and as von Harben moved across the sand he tried to find some explanation of Gabula's presence there—what errand had brought him to so dangerous a place?

The contestants had traversed but half the width of the arena returning to their cells when a sudden scream, ringing out behind them, caused them all to turn. Von Harben saw that the disturbance came from the imperial loge, but the scene that met his startled gaze seemed too preposterous to have greater substance than a dream. Perhaps it was all a dream. Perhaps there was no Castrum Mare. Perhaps there was no Validus Augustus. Perhaps there was no—ah, but that could not be true, there was a Favonia and this preposterous thing then that he was looking at was true too. He saw a man holding Cæsar by the throat and driving a dagger into his heart with the other, and the man was Gabula.

It all happened so quickly and was over so quickly that
145

scarcely had Cæsar's shriek rung through the Colosseum than he lay dead at the foot of his carved throne, and Gabula, the assassin, in a single leap had cleared the arena wall and was running across the sand toward von Harben.

"I have avenged you, Bwana!" cried Gabula. "No matter what they do to you, you are avenged."

A great groan arose from the audience and then a cheer as someone shouted: "Cæsar is dead!"

A hope flashed to the breast of von Harben. He turned and grabbed Mallius Lepus by the arm. "Cæsar is dead," he whispered. "Now is our chance."

"What do you mean?" demanded Mallius Lepus.

"In the confusion we can escape. We can hide in the city and at night we can take Favonia with us and go away."

"Where?" asked Mallius Lepus.

"God! I do not know," exclaimed von Harben, "but anywhere would be better than here, for Fulvus Fupus is Cæsar and if we do not save Favonia tonight, it will be too late."

"You are right," said Mallius Lepus.

"Pass the word to the others," said von Harben. "The more there are who try to escape the better chance there will be for some of us to succeed."

The legionaries and their officers as well as the vast multitude could attend only upon what was happening in the loge of Cæsar. So few of them had seen what really occurred there that as yet there had been no pursuit of Gabula.

Mallius Lepus turned to the other prisoners. "The gods have been good to us," he cried. "Cæsar is dead and in the confusion we can escape. Come!"

As Mallius Lepus started on a run toward the gateway that led to the cells beneath the Colosseum, the shouting prisoners fell in behind him. Only those of the professional gladiators who were freemen held aloof, but they made no effort to stop them.

"Good luck!" shouted Claudius Taurus, as von Harben passed him. "Now if someone would kill Fulvus Fupus we might have a Cæsar who is a Cæsar."

The sudden rush of the escaping prisoners so confused and upset the few guards beneath the Colosseum that they were easily overpowered and a moment later the prisoners found themselves in the streets of Castrum Mare.

"Where now?" cried one.

"We must scatter," said Mallius Lepus. "Each man for himself."

"We shall stick together, Mallius Lepus," said von Harben.

"To the end," replied the Roman.

"And here is Gabula," said von Harben, as the Negro joined them. "He shall come with us."

"We cannot desert the brave Gabula," said Mallius Lepus, "but the first thing for us to do is to find a hiding-place."

"There is a low wall across the avenue," said von Harben, "and there are trees beyond it."

"Come, then," said Mallius Lepus. "It is as good for now as any other place."

The three men hurried across the avenue and scaled the low wall, finding themselves in a garden so overgrown with weeds and underbrush that they at once assumed that it was deserted. Creeping through the weeds and forcing their way through the underbrush, they came to the rear of a house. A broken door, hanging by one hinge, windows from which the wooden blinds had fallen, an accumulation of rubbish upon the threshold marked the dilapidated structure as a deserted house.

"Perhaps this is just the place for us to hide until night," said von Harben.

"Its proximity to the Colosseum is its greatest advantage," said Mallius Lepus, "for they will be sure to believe that we have rushed as far from our dungeon as we could. Let us go in and investigate. We must be sure that the place is uninhabited."

The rear room, which had been the kitchen, had a crumbling brick oven in one corner, a bench and a dilapidated table. Crossing the kitchen, they entered an apartment beyond and saw that these two rooms constituted all that there was to the house. The front room was large and as the blinds at the windows facing the avenue had not fallen, it was dark within it. In one corner they saw a ladder reaching to a trap-door in the ceiling, which evidently led to the roof of the building, and two or three feet below the ceiling and running entirely across the end of the room where the ladder arose was a false ceiling, which formed a tiny loft just below the roof-beams, a place utilized by former tenants as a storage room. A more careful examination of the room revealed nothing more than a pile of filthy rags against one wall, the remains perhaps of some homeless beggar's bed.

"It could not have been better," said Mallius Lepus, "if this had been built for us. Why, we have three exits if we are hard pressed—one into the back garden, one into the avenue in front, and the third to the roof."

"We can remain in safety, then," said von Harben, "until after dark, when it should be easy to make our way unseen through the dark streets to the home of Septimus Favonius."

147

22

Eᴀsᴛ along the Via Mare from Castra Sanguinarius marched five thousand men. The white plumes of the Waziri
nodded at the back of Tarzan. Stalwart legionaries followed Maximus Præclarus, while the warriors of the outer
villages brought up the rear.

Sweating slaves dragged catapults, ballistæ, testudones,
huge battering-rams, and other ancient engines of war. There
were scaling ladders and wall hooks and devices for throwing
fire balls into the defenses of an enemy. The heavy engines
had delayed the march and Tarzan had chafed at the delay,
but he had to listen to Maximus Præclarus and Cassius Hasta
and Cæcilius Metellus, all of whom had assured him that
the fort, which defended the only road to Castrum Mare,
could not be taken by assault without the aid of these
mechanical engines of war.

Along the hot and dusty Via Mare the Waziri swung,
chanting the war-songs of their people. The hardened legionaries, their heavy helmets dangling against their breasts from
cords that passed about their necks, their packs on forked
sticks across their shoulders, their great oblong shields hanging in their leather covers at their backs, cursed and grumbled as become veterans, while the warriors from the outer
villages laughed and sang and chattered as might a party of
picnickers.

As they approached the fort with its moat and embankment and palisade and towers, slaves were bearing the body
of Validus Augustus to his palace within the city, and Fulvus
Fupus, surrounded by fawning sycophants, was proclaiming
himself Cæsar, though he trembled inwardly in contempla-
tion of what fate might lie before him—for though he was a
fool he knew that he was not popular and that many a noble
patrician with a strong following had a better right to the
imperial purple than he.

Throughout the city of Castrum Mare legionaries searched
for the escaped prisoners and especially for the slave
who had struck down Validus Augustus, though they were
handicapped by the fact that no one had recognized Gabula,
for there were few in the city and certainly none in the en-

tourage of Cæsar who was familiar with the face of the black from distant Urambi.

A few of the thieves and five or six gladiators, who were condemned felons and not freemen, had clung together in the break for freedom and presently they found themselves in hiding in a low part of the city, in a den where wine could be procured and where there were other forms of entertainment for people of their class.

"What sort of a Cæsar will this Fulvus Fupus make?" asked one.

"He will be worse than Validus Augustus," said another. "I have seen him in the Baths where I once worked. He is vain and dull and ignorant; even the patricians hate him."

"They say he is going to marry the daughter of Septimus Favonius."

"I saw her in the Colosseum today," said another. "I know her well by sight, for she used to come to the shop of my father and make purchases before I was sent to the dungeons."

"Have you ever been to the house of Septimus Favonius?" asked another.

"Yes, I have," said the youth. "Twice I took goods there for her inspection, going through the forecourt and into the inner garden. I know the place well."

"If one like her should happen to fall into the hands of a few poor convicts they might win their freedom and a great ransom," suggested a low-browed fellow with evil, cunning eyes.

"And be drawn asunder by wild oxen for their pains."

"We must die anyway if we are caught."

"It is a good plan."

They drank again for several minutes in silence, evidencing that the plan was milling in their minds.

"The new Cæsar should pay an enormous ransom for his bride."

The youth rose eagerly to his feet. "I will lead you to the home of Septimus Favonius and guarantee that they will open the gate for me and let me in, as I know what to say. All I need is a bundle and I can tell the slave that it contains goods that my father wishes Favonia to inspect."

"You are not such a fool as you look."

"No, and I shall have a large share of the ransom for my part in it," said the youth.

"If there is any ransom, we shall share and share alike."

Night was falling as Tarzan's army halted before the defenses of Castrum Mare. Cassius Hasta, to whom the reduction of the fort had been entrusted, disposed his forces and supervised the placing of his various engines of war.

Within the city Erich von Harben and Mallius Lepus discussed the details of their plans. It was the judgment of Lepus to wait until after midnight before making any move to leave their hiding-place.

"The streets will be deserted then," said Mallius Lepus, "except for an occasional patrol upon the principal avenue, and these may be easily eluded, since the torches that they carry proclaim their approach long before there is any danger of their apprehending us. I have the key to the gate of my uncle's garden, which insures that we may enter the grounds silently and unobserved."

"Perhaps you are right," said von Harben, "but I dread the long wait and the thought of further inaction seems unbearable."

"Have patience, my friend," said Mallius Lepus. "Fulvus Fupus will be too busy with his new Cæsarship to give heed to aught else for some time, and Favonia will be safe from him, certainly for the next few hours at least."

And as they discussed the matter, a youth knocked upon the door of the home of Septimus Favonius. Beneath the shadow of the trees along the wall darker shadows crouched. A slave bearing a lamp came to the door in answer to the knocking and, speaking through a small grille, asked who was without and what the nature of his business.

"I am the son of Tabernarius," said the youth. "I have brought fabrics from the shop of my father that the daughter of Septimus Favonius may inspect them."

The slave hesitated.

"You must remember me," said the youth. "I have been here often," and the slave held the light a little bit higher and peered through the grille.

"Yes," he said, "your face is familiar. I will go and ask my mistress if she wishes to see you. Wait here."

"These fabrics are valuable," said the youth, holding up a bundle, which he carried under his arm. "Let me stand just within the vestibule lest thieves set upon me and rob me."

"Very well, said the slave, and opening the gate he permitted the youth to enter. "Remain here until I return."

As the slave disappeared into the interior of the house, the son of Tabernarius turned quickly and withdrew the bolt that secured the door. Opening it quickly, he leaned out to voice a low signal.

Instantly the denser shadows beneath the shadowy trees moved and were resolved into the figures of men. Scurrying like vermin, they hurried through the doorway and into the home of Septimus Favonius, and into the anteroom off the vestibule the son of Tabernarius hustled them. Then he closed both doors and waited.

Presently the slave returned. "The daughter of Septimus Favonius recalls having ordered no goods from Tabernarius," he said, "nor does she feel in any mood to inspect fabrics this night. Return them to your father and tell him that when the daughter of Septimus Favonius wishes to purchase she will come herself to his shop."

Now this was not what the son of Tabernarius desired and he racked his crafty brain for another plan, though to the slave he appeared but a stupid youth, staring at the floor in too much embarrassment even to take his departure.

"Come," said the slave, approaching the door and laying hold of the bolt, "you must be going."

"Wait," whispered the youth, "I have a message for Favonia. I did not wish anyone to know it and for that reason I spoke of bringing fabrics as an excuse."

"Where is the message and from whom?" demanded the slave, suspiciously.

"It is for her ears only. Tell her this and she will know from whom it is."

The slave hesitated.

"Fetch her here," said the youth. "It will be better that no other member of the household sees me."

The slave shook his head. "I will tell her," he said, for he knew that Mallius Lepus and Erich von Harben had escaped from the Colosseum and he guessed that the message might be from one of these. As he hastened back to his mistress the son of Tabernarius smiled, for though he knew not enough of Favonia to know from whom she might reasonably expect a secret message, yet he knew there were few young women who might not, at least hopefully, expect a clandestine communication. He had not long to wait before the slave returned and with him came Favonia. Her excitement was evident as she hastened eagerly forward toward the youth.

"Tell me," she cried, "you have brought word from him."

The son of Tabernarius raised a forefinger to his lip to caution her to silence. "No one must know that I am here," he whispered, "and no ears but yours may hear my message. Send your slave away."

"You may go," said Favonia to the slave. "I will let the young man out when he goes," and the slave, glad to be dismissed, content to be relieved of responsibility, moved silently away into the shadows of a corridor and thence into that uncharted limbo into which pass slaves and other lesser people when one has done with them.

151

"Tell me," cried the girl, "what word do you bring? Where is he?"

"He is here," whispered the youth, pointing to the anteroom.

"Here?" exclaimed Favonia, incredulously.

"Yes, here," said the youth. "Come," and he led her to the door and as she approached it he seized her suddenly and, clapping a hand over her mouth, dragged her into the dark anteroom beyond.

Rough hands seized her quickly and she was gagged and bound. She heard them converse in low whispers.

"We will separate here," said one. "Two of us will take her to the place we have selected. One of you will have to leave the note for Fulvus Fupus so the palace guards will find it. The rest of you scatter and go by different routes to the deserted house across from the Colosseum. Do you know the place?"

"I know it well. Many is the night that I have slept there."

"Very well," said the first speaker, who seemed to be the leader, "now be off. We have no time to waste."

"Wait," said the son of Tabernarius, "the division of the ransom has not yet been decided. Without me you could have done nothing. I should have at least half."

"Shut up or you will be lucky if you get anything," growled the leader.

"A knife between his ribs would do him good," muttered another.

"You will not give me what I asked?" demanded the youth.

"Shut up," said the leader. "Come along now, men," and carrying Favonia, whom they wrapped in a soiled and ragged cloak, they left the home of Septimus Favonius unobserved; and as two men carried a heavy bundle through the dark shadows beneath the shadowy trees the son of Tabernarius started away in the opposite direction. . . .

A youth in soiled and ragged tunic and rough sandals approached the gates of Cæsar's palace. A legionary challenged him, holding him at a distance with the point of his pike.

"What do you loitering by the palace of Cæsar by night?" demanded the legionary.

"I have a message for Cæsar," replied the youth.

The legionary guffawed. "Will you come in or shall I send Cæsar out to you?" he demanded, ironically.

"You may take the message to him yourself, soldier," replied the other, "and if you know what is good for you, you will not delay."

The seriousness of the youth's voice finally compelled the

attention of the legionary. "Well," he demanded, "out with it. What message have you for Cæsar?"

"Hasten to him and tell him that the daughter of Septimus Favonius has been abducted and that if he hastens he will find her in the deserted house that stands upon the corner opposite the chariot entrance to the Colosseum."

"Who are you?" demanded the legionary.

"Never mind," said the youth. "Tomorrow I shall come for my reward," and he turned and sped away before the legionary could detain him.

.   .   .   .

"At this rate midnight will never come," said von Harben.

Mallius Lepus laid a hand upon the shoulder of his friend. "You are impatient, but remember that it will be safer for Favonia, as well as for us, if we wait until after midnight, for the streets now must be full of searchers. All afternoon we have heard soldiers passing. It is a miracle that they have not searched this place."

"Ps-st!" cautioned von Harben. "What was that?"

"It sounded like the creaking of the gate in front of the house," said Mallius Lepus.

"They are coming," said von Harben.

The three men seized the swords with which they had armed themselves, after they had rushed the Colosseum guard, and following a plan they had already decided upon in the event that searchers approached their hiding-place, they scaled the ladder and crept out upon the roof. Leaving the trap-door pushed slightly to one side, they listened to the sounds that were now coming from below, ready to take instant action should there be any indication that the searchers might mount the ladder to the roof.

Von Harben heard voices coming from below. "Well, we made it," said one, "and no one saw us. Here come the others now," and von Harben heard the gate creak again on its rusty hinges; then the door of the house opened and he heard several people enter.

"This is a good night's work," said one.

"Is she alive? I cannot hear her breathe."

"Take the gag from her mouth."

"And let her scream for help?"

"We can keep her quiet. She is worth nothing to us dead."

"All right, take it out."

"Listen, you, we will take the gag out of your mouth, but if you scream it will be the worse for you."

"I shall not scream," said a woman's voice in familiar tones that set von Harben's heart to palpitating, though he knew that it was nothing more than his imagination that suggested the seeming familiarity.

153

"We shall not hurt you," said a man's voice, "if you keep quiet and Cæsar sends the ransom."

"And if he does not send it?" asked the girl.

"Then, perhaps, your father, Septimus Favonius, will pay the price we ask."

"Heavens!" muttered von Harben. "Did you hear that, Lepus?"

"I heard," replied the Roman.

"Then come," whispered von Harben. "Come, Gabula, Favonia is below."

Casting discretion to the wind, von Harben tore the trap from the opening in the roof and dropped into the darkness below, followed by Mallius Lepus and Gabula.

"Favonia!" he cried. "It is I. Where are you?"

"Here," cried the girl.

Rushing blindly in the direction of her voice, von Harben encountered one of the abductors. The fellow grappled with him, while, terrified by fear that the legionaries were upon them, the others bolted from the building. As they went they left the door open and the light of a full moon dissipated the darkness of the interior, revealing von Harben struggling with a burly fellow who had seized the other's throat and was now trying to draw his dagger from its sheath.

Instantly Mallius Lepus and Gabula were upon him, and a quick thrust of the former's sword put a definite period to the earthly rascality of the criminal. Free from his antagonist, von Harben leaped to his feet and ran to Favonia, where she lay upon a pile of dirty rags against the wall. Quickly he cut her bonds and soon they had her story.

"If you are no worse for the fright," said Mallius Lepus, "we may thank these scoundrels for simplifying our task, for here we are ready to try for our escape a full three hours earlier than we had hoped."

"Let us lose no time, then," said von Harben. "I shall not breathe freely until I am across the wall."

"I believe we have little to fear now," said Mallius Lepus. "The wall is poorly guarded. There are many places where we can scale it, and I know a dozen places where we can find boats that are used by the fishermen of the city. What lies beyond is upon the knees of the gods."

Gabula, who had been standing in the doorway, closed the door quickly and crossed to von Harben. "Lights are coming down the avenue, Bwana," he said. "I think many men are coming. Perhaps they are soldiers."

The four listened intently until they made out distinctly the measured tread of marching men.

"Some more searchers," said Mallius Lepus. "When they have passed on their way, it will be safe to depart."

The light from the torches of the legionaries approached until it shone through the cracks in the wooden blinds, but it did not pass on as they had expected. Mallius Lepus put an eye to an opening in one of the blinds.

"They have halted in front of the house," he said. "A part of them are turning the corner, but the rest are remaining."

They stood in silence for what seemed a long time, though it was only a few minutes, and then they heard sounds coming from the garden behind the house and the light of torches was visible through the open kitchen door.

"We are surrounded," said Lepus. "They are coming in the front way. They are going to search the house."

"What shall we do?" cried Favonia.

"The roof is our only hope," whispered von Harben, but even as he spoke the sound of sandaled feet was heard upon the roof and the light of torches shone through the open trap.

"We are lost," said Mallius Lepus. "We cannot defeat an entire century of legionaries."

"We can fight them, though," said von Harben.

"And risk Favonia's life uselessly?" said Lepus.

"You are right," said von Harben, sadly, and then, "Wait, I have a plan. Come, Favonia, quickly. Lie down here upon the floor and I will cover you with these rags. There is no reason why we should all be taken. Mallius Lepus, Gabula, and I may not escape, but they will never guess that you are here, and when they are gone you can easily make your way to the guard-house in the Colosseum, where the officer in charge will see that you are given protection and an escort to your home."

"Let them take me," said the girl. "If you are to be captured, let me be captured also."

"It will do no good," said von Harben. "They will only separate us, and if you are found here with us it may bring suspicion upon Septimus Favonius."

Without further argument she threw herself upon the floor, resigned in the face of von Harben's argument, and he covered her over with the rags that had been a beggar's bed.

23

B Y the time that Cassius Hasta had disposed his forces and placed his engines of war before the defenses of Castrum Mare, he discovered that it was too dark to open his assault that day, but he could carry out another plan that he had and so he advanced toward the gate, accompanied by Tarzan, Metellus, and Præclarus and preceded by torch-bearers and a legionary bearing a flag of truce.

Within the fort great excitement had reigned from the moment that the advancing troops had been sighted. Word had been sent to Fulvus Fupus and reënforcements had been hurried to the fort. It was assumed by all that Sublatus had inaugurated a new raid upon a larger scale than usual, but they were ready to meet it, nor did they anticipate defeat. As the officer commanding the defenders saw the party approaching with a flag of truce, he demanded from a tower gate the nature of their mission.

"I have two demands to make upon Validus Augustus," said Cassius Hasta. "One is that he free Mallius Lepus and Erich von Harben and the other is that he permit me to return to Castrum Mare and enjoy the privileges of my station."

"Who are you?" demanded the officer.

"I am Cassius Hasta. You should know me well."

"The gods are good!" cried the officer.

"Long live Cassius Hasta! Down with Fulvus Fupus!" cried a hoarse chorus of rough voices.

Someone threw open the gates, and the officer, an old friend of Cassius Hasta, rushed out and embraced him.

"What is the meaning of all this?" demanded Cassius Hasta. "What has happened?"

"Validus Augustus is dead. He was assassinated at the games today and Fulvus Fupus has assumed the title of Cæsar. You are indeed come in time. All Castrum Mare will welcome you."

Along the Via Mare from the castle to the lakeshore and across the pontoon bridge to the island marched the army of the new Emperor of the East, while the news spread through the city and crowds gathered and shrieked their welcome to Cassius Hasta.

In a deserted house across the avenue from the Colesseum four fugitives awaited the coming of the legionaries of
Fulvus Fupus. It was evident that the soldiers intended
to take no chances. They entirely surrounded the building
and they seemed to be in no hurry to enter.

Von Harben had had ample time to cover Favonia with
the rags, so that she was entirely concealed before the
legionaries entered simultaneously from the garden, the avenue, and the roof, torch-bearers lighting their way.

"It is useless to resist," said Mallius Lepus to the officer
who accompanied the men in from the avenue. "We will
return to the dungeons peaceably."

"Not so fast," said the officer. "Where is the girl?"

"What girl?" demanded Mallius Lepus.

"The daughter of Septimus Favonius, of course."

"How should we know?" demanded von Harben.

"You abducted her and brought her here," replied the
officer. "Search the room," he commanded, and a moment
later a legionary uncovered Favonia and raised her to her
feet.

The officer laughed as he ordered the three men disarmed.

"Wait," said von Harben. "What are you going to do with
the daughter of Septimus Favonius? Will you see that she has
a safe escort to her father's house?"

"I am taking my orders from Cæsar," replied the officer.

"What has Cæsar to do with this?" demanded von Harben.

"He has ordered us to bring Favonia to the palace and
to slay her abductors upon the spot."

"Then Cæsar shall pay for us all with legionaries," cried
von Harben, and with his sword he fell upon the officer in the
doorway, while Gabula and Mallius Lepus, spurred by a similar determination to sell their lives as dearly as possible,
rushed those who were descending the ladder and entering
the kitchen door. Taken by surprise and momentarily disconcerted by the sudden and unexpected assault, the legionaries fell back. The officer, who managed to elude von
Harben's thrust, escaped from the building and summoned a
number of the legionaries who were armed with pikes.

"There are three men in that room," he said, "and a
woman. Kill the men, but be sure that the woman is not
harmed."

In the avenue the officer saw people running; heard them
shouting. He saw them stop as they were questioned by some
of his legionaries, whom he had left in the avenue. He had
not given the final order for his pike-men to enter the
building because his curiosity had momentarily distracted his
attention. As he turned now, however, to order them in,

157

his attention was again distracted by a tumult of voices that rose in great cheers and rolled up the avenue from the direction of the bridge that connects the city with the Via Mare and the fort. As he turned to look, he saw the flare of many torches and now he heard the blare of trumpets and the thud of marching feet.

What had happened? He had known, as had everyone in Castrum Mare, that the forces of Sublatus were camped before the fort, but he knew that there had been no battle and so this could not be the army of Sublatus entering Castrum Mare, but it was equally strange if the defenders of Castrum Mare should be marching away from the fort while it was menaced by an enemy army. He could not understand these things, nor could he understand why the people were cheering.

As he stood there watching the approach of the marching column, the shouts of the people took on form and he heard the name of Cassius Hasta distinctly.

"What has happened?" he demanded, shouting to the men in the street.

"Cassius Hasta has returned at the head of a big army, and Fulvus Fupus has already fled and is in hiding."

The shouted question and the equally loud reply were heard by all within the room.

"We are saved," cried Mallius Lepus, "for Cassius Hasta will harm no friend of Septimus Favonius. Aside now, you fools, if you know when you are well off," and he advanced toward the doorway.

"Back, men," cried the officer. "Back to the avenue. Let no hand be raised against Mallius Lepus or these other friends of Cassius Hasta, Emperor of the East."

"I guess this fellow knows which side his bread is buttered on," commented von Harben, with a grin.

Together Favonia, von Harben, Lepus, and Gabula stepped from the deserted building into the avenue. Approaching them they saw the head of a column of marching men; flaming torches lighted the scene until it was almost as bright as day.

"There is Cassius Hasta," exclaimed Mallius Lepus. "It is indeed he, but who are those with him?"

"They must be Sanguinarians," said Favonia. "But look, one of them is garbed like a barbarian, and see the strange warriors with their white plumes that are marching behind them."

"I have never seen the like in all my life," exclaimed Mallius Lepus.

"Neither have I," said von Harben, "but I am sure that I

recognize them, for their fame is great and they answer the description that I have heard a thousand times."

"Who are they?" asked Favonia.

"The white giant is Tarzan of the Apes, and the warriors are his Waziri fighting men."

At sight of the legionaries standing before the house, Cassius Hasta halted the column.

"Where is the centurion in command of these troops?" he demanded.

"It is I, glorious Cæsar," replied the officer, who had come to arrest the abductors of Favonia.

"Does it happen that you are one of the detachments sent out by Fulvus Fupus to search for Mallius Lepus and the barbarian, von Harben?"

"We are here, Cæsar," cried Mallius Lepus, while Favonia, von Harben, and Gabula followed behind him.

"May the gods be praised!" exclaimed Cassius Hasta, as he embraced his old friend. "But where is the barbarian chieftain from Germania, whose fame has reached even to Castra Sanguinarius?"

"This is he," said Mallius Lepus. "This is Erich von Harben."

Tarzan stepped nearer. "You are Erich von Harben?" he asked in English.

"And you are Tarzan of the Apes, I know," returned von Harben, in the same language.

"You look every inch a Roman," said Tarzan with a smile.

"I feel every inch a barbarian, however," grinned von Harben.

"Roman or barbarian, your father will be glad when I bring you back to him."

"You came here in search of me, Tarzan of the Apes?" demanded von Harben.

"And I seemed to have arrived just in time," said the ape-man.

"How can I ever thank you?" exclaimed von Harben.

"Do not thank me, my friend," said the ape-man. "Thank little Nkima!"

The End

About Edgar Rice Burroughs

Edgar Rice Burroughs is one of the world's most popular authors. With no previous experience as an author, he wrote and sold his first novel—*A Princess of Mars*—in 1912. In the ensuing thirty-eight years until his death in 1950, Burroughs wrote 91 books and a host of short stories and articles. Although best known as the creator of the classic *Tarzan of the Apes* and *John Carter of Mars,* his restless imagination knew few bounds. Burroughs' prolific pen ranged from the American West to primitive Africa and on to romantic adventure on the moon, the planets, and even beyond the farthest star.

No one knows how many copies of ERB books have been published throughout the world. It is conservative to say, however, that of the translations into 32 known languages, including Braille, the number must run into the hundreds of millions. When one considers the additional world-wide following of the Tarzan newspaper feature, radio programs, comic magazines, motion pictures and television, Burroughs must have been known and loved by literally a thousand million or more.